STORIES BUILT
TO **LAST**

abbycat group

&

PUBLISHING
BRANDS

S I N C E   2 0 2 5

www.abbycatgroup.com

OVERTIME

AGP

JACK CHASE

BLACK

OVERTIME

THE **BALLAD**
OF **MARCUS GRAVES**

Published by Abbycat Black
An imprint of Abbycat Group LLC, operating as AGP | Abbycat Group & Publishing Brands
Palm Desert, California
www.abbycatgroup.com

ISBN 979-8-9986388-0-0 (Paperback)
ISBN 979-8-9986388-1-7 (eBook)

Cover design by FRAMEWORKS
Book design by FRAMEWORKS
Text set in EB Garamond

First edition, April 2025

Printed in the United States of America

10 9 8 7 6 5 4 3 2 1

For my late father, Darrick Chase.

Thank you for being my fiercest supporter, the funniest and most patient man I've ever known, and the rock who always had Mom, Sam, and me covered.

I love you, Dad.

"I wanted the whole world or nothing."

Charles Bukowski

THE CLOCK

1

THE REAL SIN CITY

Want to know how much the Mexican drug trade generates per year?

Half a trillion.

That's five hundred billion dollars, *netted*.

There was a time when the Mexican drug trade was worth more than Amazon. The kicker?

That's just to America.

Welcome to the real Sin City: Los Angeles, California, where the palm trees are imported and the souls are sold wholesale. From the drug-addled starlets with thousand-yard stares to the soulless social climbers measuring their worth in Instagram followers, an unwritten mantra underlies this sun-bleached, capitalistic cesspit of glorified decadence and God complexes: you're a star, or you're not. You want to be in the movies? Get a bartending job and slug your way through auditions with the ten thousand other beautiful faces that arrived on the same Greyhound from Nowhere, USA. Next Chris Farley? Take your lumps at The Comedy Store while the ghosts of legends past judge your punchlines. You develop your material, your sound, your reason. Your fucking *why*.

In short? You handle your shit.

I never liked school. I figured nobody else did either: just another necessary evil of modern existence, like taxes or your girlfriend's friends. I went and got my AA anyway. Bucks County Community College. High school had been a waste of time. The friends I had either dropped out or might as well have. Because I'm a glutton for punishment, I chose Pre-law. Specifically?

Criminal Justice.

I'd studied criminal law the way other kids studied batting averages: obsessively, hungrily, like it held the secret to something I couldn't name yet. Constitutional amendments, Miranda rights, the precise choreography of evidence chains. I memorized it all with the dedication of a monk copying scripture, never quite admitting to myself why. Maybe because understanding the rules meant understanding how power really worked—who had it, who didn't, and the thin line between the hunters and the hunted.

I always wanted to be in California. The Golden State. The promised land. They just happened to give me a scholarship. Like I said, I never liked school. But I could do it as good as anybody.

I grew up in a weird part of Philly. Not poor, not rich, not even really middle-class, just kind of right there on the edge, in the kind of neighborhood where hope and resignation fight daily turf wars on porches with peeling paint. My dad, William Graves, was a mechanic with oil-stained fingernails no amount of Lava soap could touch, a wardrobe consisting entirely of tucked-in short-sleeve button-downs, buckled slacks, and the same pair of brown leather shoes he'd been resoling since Clinton was in office —a man from another era. Short-haired, scruffy, medium build, with a general air of decency that seemed to fade a little more each year, like a photograph left too long in the sun.

"Marcus, gimme a hand with some of these bags," he called from the driveway one morning when I was ten, his voice gruff from the three Camels he'd already smoked.

I walked out to the '80 Impala. The trunk was open. Groceries.

"You like sprouts?" he asked, squinting against the morning light, a fourth cigarette tucked behind his ear for later.

I shrugged.

"Take these in for your old man." He stuck two paper bags, ready to pop at the seams, in my tiny arms. Then he reached into the back of the trunk and slid a fifth of whiskey into the side of one of them, the amber liquid catching the sunlight. "This, too. Don't let your mother see you. Top cabinet next to the stove. There's a Milky Way in it for you."

I smiled at the mention of chocolate and teetered back inside with the overstuffed bags. I climbed onto a stepping stool, my small hands carefully hiding my father's bottle behind a loaf of bread and some Pop-Tart boxes, already learning the choreography of family secrets. Even at ten, I understood the transaction perfectly. Silence for sugar. Complicity for candy. It wasn't corruption. Corruption implies innocence lost. This was education. My father was teaching me the fundamental law of family dynamics: everyone has secrets, everyone has prices, and the smart money learns both early.

My dad didn't make enough and he knew it. The knowledge sat on his shoulders like an invisible weight, bending him a little more each year. After all, his father's life insurance had paid off the house. He didn't get to go to college. Instead, he worked at his dad's auto-body in North Philly, inhaling metal dust and exhaust fumes six days a week. Once he turned twenty-four, it became his. He was a good man, a hard worker with hands that told stories of labor his mouth never would. And I was happy.

Until it became hard to be.

I was lying in bed one night, counting the glow-in-the-dark stars my father had helped me stick to the ceiling years before. A door slammed downstairs. Muffled voices rose like smoke through the floorboards. A fight brewing.

I tiptoed out of my room, heart pounding against my ribs.

I spied from behind the stair railing, small fingers gripping the wooden bars. My father stumbled past my mother, his body swaying.

"I fucked up, Barbs. I'm sorry." His words slurred together, each syllable tripping over the next.

My mother, Barbara Graves, born and raised by a cop and four brothers in Paterson, New Jersey, stood arms crossed and jaw set, striking and hard-eyed with pulled-back black hair that seemed to stretch her face tight.

"Yeah, Bill. You fucked up. You *are* a fuck-up." I always remembered her inflection when she was *truly* angry: calm, precise, and far more frightening than any screaming fit. I can still see her standing there in her robe with her curlers in.

"It was Richard, he—" My father's hand grasped at the wall for support.

"*Fuck* Richard. You know what, Billy? I'm tempted to wrangle that boy down here and just get it over with. For Christ's sake, you smell like a pack of Reds, you look like you crawled through a sewer, you can't even *walk* straight—"

"I'm gonna sleep down here." He wandered into the living room, lost in his own home.

"No shit. Think you're getting in my bed?" She stomped back upstairs, each step an exclamation point.

I scattered back into my room, diving under covers that smelled of fabric softener and childhood.

Later, thirst pulled me from bed, and I tried to silently cross the minefield of creaky floorboards toward the kitchen for water.

"Marcus..." William sensed me nonetheless, like animals sense earthquakes before they hit. He was laid out on the couch, a beached drunk swatting at invisible seagulls like they were creditors.

I slowly approached him, my small feet hesitant on the carpet, staring with innocent eyes that still believed fathers were heroes.

"Why are you up?" His words were clearer now, as if the importance of speaking to his son had temporarily burned away some of the alcohol fog.

"Just getting water," I said, my voice thin in the darkness.

"There's bottles in the garage." He gestured vaguely toward the door.

"Okay," I said, turning to leave. "Good night, Dad."

"C'mere. Chat with your old man." The request sounded like a plea, even to my young ears.

I hesitated, caught between childish obedience and newfound wariness, then took a seat at his feet.

"Untie those for me, would ya?" He lifted a foot slightly, the effort visible.

I untied his boots: heavy, steel-toed monsters that smelled of oil and man-sweat. He kicked them off with a dull thud against the carpet.

"Look, if something funny happens between me and your mother... don't feel bad, okay?" He paused, searching for words in the darkness as if they were stars. "She's an amazing woman..." His voice took on a reverence reserved for things just out of reach. "I want you to always be her protector. I don't want you to be like me. I didn't," he swallowed hard, "have the guts to go out in the world, make something of my own. I want you to stake your own claim. Whatever it is, do it right. And when you find your opportunity, take it. 'Cause if you don't, somebody else will. And that's more guaranteed than any kind of failure you'll ever face. I love you, kid. You know that, right?" His eyes searched mine, hungry for affirmation.

I remained there with my father in the dark, the silence punctuated only by the wall clock counting down moments we'd never get back, as he drifted back into a drunken slumber. His breathing settled into the ragged rhythm of the defeated, and I realized something that would follow me to California and beyond: this was what love looked like when it ran out of options. Desperate and drunk and trying to pass wisdom to a kid who'd rather be sleeping. He loved me enough to warn me, even through a whiskey haze. Loved me enough to name his failures so I might avoid them. Most people think love is about protection. They're wrong. Love is about *preparation*. Teaching someone to survive the world, even if it means surviving you.

At the time, I didn't really know what the fuck the guy was talking about. But as I grew up, I always thought back to it. He was right. I *didn't* want to be like him: a man whose dreams had calcified into resignation, whose ambitions had been drowned one liquor store transaction at a time. I knew there had to be something else out there. Something incredible, maybe. I just didn't know what. But I knew one thing with bone-deep certainty: I wouldn't be bound. Not by anything, or anybody.

They divorced six months later.

I remember sitting in a high-backed leather chair in a sterile law office, legs dangling above the carpet, reading a dog-eared copy of *The Hardy Boys* while my mom spoke to her lawyer in a glass-paneled conference room. They laughed and seemingly flirted, though I couldn't hear a word through the glass. Her face looked younger there, lighter.

I don't blame her for seeking escape from a sinking ship, but she could've been a little less gleeful about it. Less like a prisoner seeing daylight and more like someone mourning the death of something that once mattered. But that's not how people work. We're wired for escape, not elegies. Barbara Graves had spent years in emotional maximum security, and the day she walked into that lawyer's office was the day she tasted freedom for the first time in, well, forever. The rational part of me understood. The ten-year-old part still wanted her to cry. Still wanted *some* evidence that our little family's dissolution hurt her as much as it was about to hurt me. But that would've required her to mourn something she'd stopped believing in years ago. And nobody mourns a ghost.

She exited the conference room, laughing and smiling, her perfume announcing her arrival seconds before she appeared. The lawyer followed her out: tall, silver-haired, with the confident stride of a man who'd never doubted his place in the world.

"Coffee, then?" he asked, his voice smooth as polished marble.

"That would be great," my mother said, tucking a strand of hair behind her ear in a gesture I'd never seen before. "This is my son, Marcus."

"Nice looking boy. Takes after his mother." His teeth were impossibly white as he extended his hand. "I'm Ed."

I stared at his hand coldly, my father's sadness a phantom limb I carried. An icy beat passed between us. Ed's face turned red, hand retreating back into his pocket as if bitten. He pivoted, shifting his attention back to my mother like a sunflower tracking light.

"Tuesday, then."

"Thank you for everything, Ed."

She grabbed my hand, her tone snapping from sweet to bossy, and dragged me toward the elevator.

"Why didn't you say hi?" she hissed under her breath.

"I don't know," I mumbled, though I did know. I just couldn't name it yet.

"Well, it's not how I taught you. Alright, we gotta move. I have a job interview in thirty minutes."

"Can we get ice cream?" I asked.

"I'm making dinner in two hours. What do you want ice cream for?"

"Dad always gets it for me. Even before dinner." I wielded his name like a weapon, watching it hit its mark.

"Your father does a lot of things," she snapped. "Man has no sense of boundaries."

"Boundaries?"

She hit the elevator button with unnecessary force before kneeling to my eye level: "Listen to me, Marcus. Your father's not a good man. He's *sick*, you understand?"

"Daddy's sick?"

"In a way. Yes." Her voice softened, almost pitying.

We got into the elevator, and the doors closed with quiet finality, cueing my next decade around the sun.

California was a turning point for me. A clean slate.

And Billy Graves's drunken prophecy was about to come true in ways neither of us could have imagined.

2

BUDDY

The campus sprawled like a postcard dream: all red-tiled roofs and bougainvillea-covered walkways under an impossibly blue sky. I sat at a desk about six levels up in a lecture hall that smelled of floor polish and ambition, twiddling a pencil between fingers that couldn't quite settle. The brand-new chalkboard read criminal justice in the handwriting of someone who took themselves very seriously.

Professor Dylan Crabtree, tweedy and bow-tied like a parody of academia, droned on and on about something that couldn't compete with the California sunshine pouring through the windows, much less get him laid. I scribbled in my notebook, doodles masquerading as notes.

Then the door swung open, theatrical and unapologetic.

Buddy Reyes, an energetic, pompous nineteen-year-old Latino with the swagger of someone who'd never faced consequences that money couldn't make disappear. A stained-yellow Chinese take-out box steamed in one hand and a beaten-up textbook dangled from the other. He slugged his way up the stairs in a bright-green bomber jacket that probably cost more than my entire wardrobe, grinning like he owned the place. Maybe his family did, for all I knew.

"Mr. Reyes, care to make another excuse?" Professor Crabtree sighed with the weary resignation of a man who'd seen this movie before and didn't like the ending.

"You know, I would, Dylan, but it ain't that complicated." He held up the box like Exhibit A in his defense. "The line was just so damn long. I mean, it's like Chinese New Year in that motherfucker."

I couldn't help but laugh at Buddy's audaciousness: the casual disrespect, the boundary-crossing first-name basis, the theatrical explanation. It was like watching someone walk a tightrope without a net, but with the confidence of someone who didn't believe in falling.

"That'll be another write-up and a trip to the Dean's office for you, Mr. Reyes," Crabtree said as Buddy found a seat beside me, drawn to my laughter like a moth to flame.

"Don't hold it against me, Big D. Man's gotta eat!" Buddy glanced at me with the complicity of a co-conspirator and signaled to his now-opened box of chow mein, rice, and orange chicken. The smell wafted up like a siren's call. "You want a bite? Couldn't just let you smell it. I ain't that evil."

I politely refused, though my empty stomach protested. Buddy gestured toward the Professor with his fork, a king granting audience to a peasant.

"How 'bout this fucking guy? You believe him?" His voice was pitched perfectly between amusement and disdain.

I shrugged, not yet ready to declare allegiances in this classroom drama. Buddy smiled, a flash of white teeth like a shark's warning, and outstretched his hand.

"Buddy Reyes."

"Marcus," I replied, my own name suddenly sounding insufficient next to his.

We shook hands, his grip firm and dry. We became friends. What I didn't know then was that friendship with guys like Buddy isn't really friendship at all. It's recruitment. They don't befriend you; they audition you. Every laugh you share, every confidence you exchange, every moment of genuine connection is actually a job interview disguised as camaraderie. And I was interviewing beautifully. Laughing at his jokes, impressed by his swagger, hungry for whatever world he represented. I thought I was making a friend. He knew he was making an asset.

A few days later, we walked along Santa Monica Pier. The Pacific stretched out before us, vast and impossibly blue, making promises neither of us understood yet. Tourists milled about with their oversized cameras and undersized attention spans, collecting memories they'd bore friends with back home. The scent of funnel cakes and salt water hung in the air like something from a better life.

"Last time I brought a girl here, a bird shit on her head," Buddy said, flicking a cigarette butt over the railing with practiced nonchalance, watching it arc toward the water below.

"Was that the first and only?" I asked, leaning against the weathered wood railing.

"Actually, we dated for three months."

"Did you laugh?" I couldn't help asking, already knowing the answer.

"Of course I fucking laughed. Once she went into the bathroom." He slapped the railing. "Girl comes back with wet hair, thinking she washed it all out. Had a white streak like fucking Rogue from X-Men."

We both laughed, the sound carried away by the ocean breeze. For a moment, we were just two college kids without complication.

"How long have you been here?" I asked, squinting against the California sun that still felt foreign on my East Coast skin.

"Off-and-on my whole life. You?" His casual claim to this golden place made my own arrival seem even more recent, more tentative.

"First time."

"Yeah, I could tell. You've still got that shiny look in your eye." He stopped walking, his attention suddenly focused entirely on me. "Philly, right?"

"Born and raised." I straightened slightly, a reflexive pride in my roots.

"That's a switch. Why here?"

"Because I heard this is where lives change." The words sounded both earnest and naive as they left my mouth.

"And school... Law, right?" He changed directions smoothly, like a shark circling.

"How'd you know that?" I asked, surprised.

"Saw a book in your bag about as thick as a Redwood." He mimed staggering under a heavy weight. "Only pre-law students carry shit like that. Medical students have tablets. Business majors have their daddies' checkbooks."

"Testing the waters, I guess." I shrugged.

"Good for you..." He said it without mockery, but with the slight condescension of someone who'd never had to work for anything watching someone who had to work for everything.

A seagull squawked in the distance.

"Let's get outta here," Buddy suggested, already bored with the scenic beauty that still amazed me. "This place is for tourists and first dates. I know somewhere we can get drinks without ID."

That's what money does. It makes you immune to wonder. When you've never had to fight for anything, nothing feels worth fighting for. But I wasn't ready to be that jaded yet. Part of me still wanted to lean against this railing and pretend I was in a movie about transformation and second chances. Another part of me (the part that was already learning to survive Buddy's world) knew that staying starry-eyed in Los Angeles was like staying naive in Vegas. A sure way to lose everything you came with.

I followed, already sensing that following Buddy Reyes would become a habit.

One rainy afternoon, a rarity in LA that brought with it unexpected homesickness, I was sitting at my desk, staring at a computer screen filled with words that had long since stopped making sense. The raindrops raced each other down the window pane, betting on futures as uncertain as my own. The door burst open without warning, and Buddy entered like a conquistador, hiding something behind his back.

"Yo, Graves," he announced, rain glistening in his dark hair like tiny diamonds.

"Hey, man," I said without looking up, pretending interest in my textbook's dissection of criminal statutes.

The charade ended when Buddy dropped a tightly wrapped pound of marijuana onto the desk with a thump that seemed to echo my heartbeat. I looked at him and frowned at this green intruder in my academic sanctuary.

"What the hell is this?"

"It's weed, the fuck you think it is?" His grin split his face with mischievous glee.

"You're gonna smoke this?"

"I'm gonna sell it."

"Why?"

"Shit, maybe I'm trying to do something for myself."

"Slinging pot like a jackass?"

Buddy assumed a seat in a neighboring chair with the fluidity of someone completely at ease in his own skin, flashing a mischievous smile that carried hints of danger.

"There's a lot more where this came from." The words hung in the air like smoke.

I paused, the implications crystallizing slowly, like ice forming on a pond. "Wait, you want me to help you? Seriously? I'm a future law student. This isn't for me."

"Relax. You think you're gonna sling an eighth and the ATF's gonna be kicking down your door with a SWAT team?" He laughed, the sound rich with privilege and the confidence of someone who'd never seen consequences. "Doesn't work like that."

"So you know how it works?" I challenged.

"Look, it's fifteen hundred in your pocket for a couple weeks of work. I wouldn't be coming to you if I didn't think you could do it."

I chewed on that for a beat, my fingers already reaching for the package, feeling its weight, its potential. I began to examine the weed with a detachment that felt practiced, professional even. The tightly compressed buds were sticky with resin, the scent strong enough to punch through the industrial-grade plastic. My fingers moved with an authority I didn't know I possessed, breaking off a small bud and rolling it between my thumb and forefinger. The texture was foreign but somehow familiar. Like muscle memory from a life I'd never lived. This wasn't oregano in a baggie sold behind the gymnasium.

This was serious merchandise. Compressed. Cured. Deliberate. I found myself calculating: weight, quality, street value, profit margins. Numbers dancing in my head like they'd been waiting there all along, hibernating until the right opportunity woke them up.

"Where'd you find this shit anyway?" I asked.

"My cousin's in town. It's a gift. That's all," Buddy explained later as we sat in a sleepy burger joint, the fluorescent lights lending his skin a jaundiced glow.

"Your cousin just randomly gives you pounds of weed?"

"Grows it with his boy in New Mexico. It's nothing." He dismissed the felony with a wave of his hand, as if discussing borrowing a sweater.

"That reminds me. Your family. What is it they do exactly?" I probed.

Buddy frowned, just a slight downward turn of lips that had been smiling seconds before. "You mean my cousin?"

"C'mon, everyone knows your folks are filthy rich. How? Oil, energy? Construction?" I pressed, leaning forward. "I feel like, in that case, your cousin would be managing a portfolio, not growing bud in a border town."

"If you already know the answer, why don't you tell me?" His eyes had gone flat, mirrors rather than windows.

"I don't think so. Spit it out." Something in me needed to hear it from his mouth, as if that would make whatever came next his responsibility instead of mine.

A sly smile formed across Buddy's face, slow and deliberate as a cat stretching in the sun.

"Fine. Let's just say we move shit. Expensive, in-demand shit. And we happen to do well. Very well." The admission was delivered with a pride that bordered on arrogance.

I held Buddy's eyes across the plastic tabletop, torn between fascination and the warning bells clanging in my head. This was the moment. The fork in the road, the decision point. Everything that came after would be shaped by what I decided in these greasy booth seats under buzzing lights.

"Look, it's not guaranteed but, my dad needs more distributors in LA. He might be tapping me. My cousin, his guy... They're good, but they got a lot on their plate. And things could always be better." His words painted a picture of opportunity wrapped in danger.

"And what makes you think we'd be any better?" The "we" slipped out, already including myself in whatever scheme he was hatching.

"We're fresh out of the box. And we have reach. Reach meets accessibility. And accessibility meets growth." He sounded like he was pitching a startup rather than a drug operation.

"I don't know, man. I don't think this is the right fit."

"Listen. Right now, we're two nobodies. But you and I, we could take over this campus. Some of these kids have their parents' money coming out of their ears. They don't care, man. They just want to get high. And we can supply that." He paused, letting the vision sink in before delivering his coup de grâce. "Do you remember what you said to me the first day we met?"

I sighed and set my fork down.

"I asked you... 'Marcus, why here? Why LA?' And you said, 'Because I heard this is where lives change.' I thought it was corny as shit at the time, but now it rings true."

"Why me?" The question was barely audible, almost rhetorical.

"'Cause you came here to *be* somebody." His eyes locked onto mine, seeing something I couldn't yet recognize in myself. "So, do you want to take care of yourself? Or do you want to just be like everybody else?"

I didn't say anything. The silence stretched between us. Buddy wiped his mouth and dropped the napkin onto his finished plate.

"We'll talk tomorrow. Besides..." He stood up, slamming a twenty onto the table with unnecessary force. "Who the fuck wants to be a lawyer anyway?"

With that, Buddy split, the door swinging behind him like a pendulum marking the passage between before and after. A beat passed in his absence, the restaurant sounds rushing in to fill the vacuum he'd left. I slurped down the last of my soda and glanced out the window at the passing traffic, each headlight a potential customer, each car a mobile marketplace.

A fuse had been lit inside me. I could feel it burning toward something explosive.

And so I sat there in that fluorescent tomb, watching traffic through grease-stained glass, and realized something fundamental had shifted. The Marcus who'd arrived in California six months ago, that earnest kid with law school dreams and a work-study job, was fading not like a photograph left in the sun, but like one of those Polaroids in time travel movies that just go away when someone fucks the wrong girl—or maybe the right one—on prom night. Maybe he was already gone, something harder and sharper crystallizing in his place.

Buddy hadn't corrupted me; corruption implies innocence destroyed. He'd simply shown me what I was capable of becoming when someone removed the safety rails. And the most terrify-ing part? I liked the view. Liked the weight of possibility in my hands, the taste of easy money on my tongue. The question wasn't whether I'd take Buddy's offer.

The question was how long I'd pretend I hadn't already decided.

3

THE MAGICIAN

Before I knew it, I was bagging everything from eighths to ounces in my dorm room, the process becoming second nature. The scale's digital readout blinked at me accusingly as I parceled out someone's weekend high, someone else's night of bad decisions, and someone else's possession charge. Buddy weighed clumps of marijuana beside me, his fingers nimble with the practiced precision of a jeweler handling loose diamonds.

"What's our base anyway?" I asked, sealing a Ziploc bag with careful pressure. "You know, what kind of people are we looking for?"

"That's your job," he replied without looking up, his focus absolute.

"Why not reach out to your folks?" The question had been bothering me: if his family was so connected, why was *he* playing small-time college dealer?

Buddy's hands stilled for just a moment, a brief glitch in his rhythm. "You don't know my old man."

The four words carried weight that kept me from asking more. Buddy's hands resumed their plucking and placing, but something in his posture had shifted, like a door slamming shut on a room I wasn't supposed to see inside.

Whatever hold Diego Reyes had over his son wasn't just paternal authority. It was something darker, more binding. I'd learned enough about family dynamics to recognize the signs: fear masquerading as respect, love twisted into obligation, the kind of relationship where disappointment didn't just hurt feelings—it had consequences.

I needed connections to make this work. In class one day, I met Ricky Atwater, a twenty-year-old with sharp looks and rough edging that suggested he'd lived more than most. The young female TA droned at the front of the half-empty classroom, her enthusiasm inversely proportional to the students' engagement.

"You know anybody here?" I asked quietly, scanning the scattered occupants of the lecture hall.

He snorted. "Her, for starters," he said, pointing to the TA.

"How?"

"Boy, I beat the breaks off that bitch." His eyes slid across the room like searchlights, landing on another target. "And this goofy motherfucker over here..." He pointed to a curly-haired ginger a few rows down, slouched so far in his seat he was practically horizontal. "We called him 'Little John' in high school. Caught whacking in Environmental Science of all fucking places. Chick who saw it put herself through, like, three months of counseling."

"Just because she saw it?"

"She said it looked like an expired Twinkie, man," he said, his laughter a short, sharp bark that drew a few scowls.

"Twinkies don't expire, though." The pedantic correction slipped out before I could stop it.

"Huh. I never thought about that." Ricky looked at me with newfound respect. "You a smart motherfucker. Point stands, though—homie's dick was mutated."

"What happened to him?" I asked, invested despite myself.

"Suspended," Ricky said, almost glum. "Off-record, sit-down with the parents type shit. What are you gonna do, you know?"

"Right," I agreed, slowly nodding as if I was absorbing the lessons of this high conversation. Then I struck: "Anything interesting happen around here?"

"You came to the right place, playboy," Ricky whispered, grinning like a shark. "AGO, GZ, APhi... Shit, I'll take you anywhere. Take down my number after this."

Word spread through campus like a virus. Soon, my phone would start ringing at all hours, the display lighting up with numbers I didn't recognize but quickly learned to anticipate, and before I knew it, I had an address book. Buddy projected we'd sell the pound in two weeks.

Ricky and I did it in one.

Like in retail, you had your demographics.

At the top were your archetypal Angelenos and their afternoon eighths. They'd pull up in gleaming Audis or BMWs wearing loosely-fitted Henleys and smelling like a scent rack, designer sunglasses blunting their foggy-eyed gazes of privilege. They were frequent, predictable, and the easiest—for me, at least—to get along with.

Then there were your usual suspects. The skate rats, the burnouts, the ones who'd been high since sophomore year and would likely stay that way until their first heart attack at forty. Devil-eyed white kids with skateboards cracking paperbagged tall boys in the shade of campus infrastructure that had paid to *avoid* them with their shrill laughter and jerky movements and failed kickflips heard across the zip code. They bought the cheap stuff, haggled over dollar increments, but always came back—because that's who they were. I tolerated them the way a shark tolerates the pilot fish that pick its teeth.

And your party girls. Sorority sisters who moved in packs, their leather purses hiding more than just pepper spray and *Plan B*.

I'd trade them bags through the window of my car for crumpled twenties, watch them wave goodbye with perfectly manicured fingers and giggle as they scattered into black Escalades that would ferry them to clubs where they'd make less formal transactions for different products. I processed them like a high-speed toll booth on the 405.

But these people weren't different—not really. Beneath the varied exteriors of put-on wealth or want, youth or fading beauty, they all wanted the same thing, and it wasn't just to get high. They wanted an experience. A release. An escape hatch from the grinding machinery of daily life. We weren't selling drugs—we were selling *happiness*, or at least its closest chemical approximation. That five minutes when your heart slows, and nothing else matters but the person standing in front of you. When the edges of the world blur just enough that you can pretend the center will hold.

The psychology was intoxicating in its own right. Every transaction was a tiny theater of human need, and I'd become both director and audience. I'd watch someone's shoulders relax the moment their fingers closed around a baggie. I'd see the gratitude flash across their face not for the product, but for the promise it represented, the temporary amnesty from whatever war they were fighting inside their own heads. I started cataloging these micro-expressions like a behavioral scientist, filing away the particular desperation that lived behind the expensive sunglasses and lip gloss, the way money changed hands with the reverence usually reserved for sacraments.

It's like an illusion. But any magician worth their top hat will tell you the hardest part about creating a good illusion isn't the method, setup, or even the execution.

It's not fucking it up.

***

One night, Buddy and me were led into a slick white suite at the Beverly Hills Waldorf by a leather jacket-clad and absurdly tall Mexican bodyguard who looked like he'd been built to survive a direct hit from a semi-truck, and was currently annoyed that one hadn't hit him yet. We'll call him Alejandro.

Another man, this one in a charcoal two-piece suit, roughly escorted a young escort in a glittery cocktail dress into the hotel corridor as she accosted him in rapid-fire Spanish. We walked past them, our reflections stretching across the wide, glossy floor of the entrance hall and into the main room where four men sat on a white leather couch that was taut and unresponsive, the kind of high-end furniture designed to be looked at rather than sat in. Beer bottles, cigarette butts, and remnants of an ongoing coke binge lay strewn all over a glass coffee table.

My eyes instinctively settled on the two anchors. Buddy's cousin, Luis Reyes, was a rangy guy with long black hair and a lean stature that suggested either athleticism or a chemically-assisted lack of hunger. Beside him sat Santiago Dominguez, a big guy with black holes for pupils who commanded the room without a word. He smoked a cigarette with deliberate slowness, his gaze fixed on me with the relaxed intensity of a predator assessing if I was prey worth digesting.

First, Luis stood to embrace his cousin.

"Buddy-Buddy. How you doin'?"

"Good," Buddy replied, looking a bit flush in the company of his version of extended family. It reminded me of that shy, out-of-place feeling I'd had at eleven visiting my father's white trash brothers and sisters for Thanksgiving: wine-box-drinking and Parliament-flicking blowhards who'd taken him in after the divorce. That was the day I learned how to swear.

Luis clicked his tongue. "Let me introduce you."

Luis introduced Buddy to Santiago. After exchanging niceties in their native tongue, Santiago gestured for Buddy to make himself at home beside him. They talked a little more in Spanish, the language creating a wall between me and whatever was being discussed. I silently, maybe awkwardly, observed the pair from just a few steps away, feeling like a kid at the grown-ups' table who'd been told to keep his mouth shut. I caught fragments: *hermano, negocio, problemas*. Brother, business, problems. The universal vocabulary of family enterprises that operated on levels greater than whether Randy Graves had gotten Ketel One or Tito's. Buddy's body language had changed *completely* in Santiago's presence, the brash swagger replaced by something more careful and deferential. It was like watching an actor drop character between scenes, revealing the person underneath the performance.

Santiago Dominguez—I would later learn—was born an orphan in Mexico City, raised in the streets, and had become, through a sequential mixture of brutality, utter abandonment of morals, and the kind of intelligence you acquire in alleyways rather than books, one of the most powerful and feared men in the drug trade. He and Buddy's cousin Luis had met at a club in Miami around '07. Buddy's father, Diego Reyes, had taken a shine to Santiago and appointed him head of American relations with Luis beside him.

He exchanged a few more words with Buddy before he shifted his hard gaze to me.

"And you are?" The question was deceptively casual, like a snake's lazy flick of the tongue before striking.

"Apologies, *señor*, I—" Buddy began, but Santiago shut him down with a look that could have frozen fire.

"Take a seat," he said to me directly.

I struggled to bury my jitters, to put on an impassive poker face that wouldn't reveal the fear crawling up my spine like something with legs.

"I'm Marcus," I managed, the words feeling inadequate in the face of his presence.

"I know," he said, almost a whisper.

I sat opposite him, adjusting my jacket in a nervous gesture I immediately regretted.

"Tell me about this... operation my partner can't stop crowing over." His tone suggested he already knew the answer but wanted to hear me deliver it. The universal test of resolve.

"Well, it's not much," I began, trying to downplay our success out of some instinctive caution. "But in the time—"

"Your numbers?" he interrupted, uninterested in my modesty.

"About five thousand dollars."

"About five thousand dollars or five thousand dollars?"

"Four thousand, nine hundred and thirteen." It sounded pitiful now.

"And your market?"

"Mostly students."

"College kids."

"*Rich* college kids," I corrected, finally locating my spine.

Santiago smiled for the first time.

"And where did you sell to these *gringos*?"

"We kept it local. Campus, housing areas. That sort of thing."

He nodded as if that made perfect sense. His eyes dipped—a piece of lint on his knee. He flicked it.

"Your parents. Where are they?"

The abrupt change of subject caught me off guard in a way that almost made me choke on whatever saliva remained in my throat. I answered quick—maybe too quick, both in timing and delivery, like an eighth grader rushing through lines in a school play.

"My mother, she lives in Philly still. And my father, he—"

"Lives in Maryland now, doesn't he? Government housing. Not much of a go-getter."

The casual display of detailed knowledge about my family was expected, even unremarkable, but still nauseating. These gentlemen had done a background check on me like I was applying for security clearance, not slinging eighths to half-lobotomized sorority girls.

Finally, words came. "Yeah. That's right."

Santiago nodded and lit another cigarette with a gold lighter, the flame briefly illuminating the planes of his face. I shot Buddy a look, but he was studiously avoiding my gaze.

"Are you close with him? Your father."

"Not really. He's a drunk. And my mother, we don't talk much." The easiest answer I've given all night, though the admission stung my heart.

He nodded. "I didn't have a father."

"I'm sorry," I said automatically, falling back on social niceties in the absence of knowing what else to say.

"Don't be. He was a junkie. A *desgracia*." He studied me. "Why did you come here, Marcus?"

"I don't understand."

"You study law, yes?" Another question he already knew the answer to.

"That's right."

"Perhaps that's a more worthy pursuit."

"Depends on how you look at it."

"What do you want, Marcus?"

"What?"

"What... do... you... want?" He spoke slowly, as if to a child or an idiot.

"I'd like to be useful." It felt stupid upon leaving my lips.

His lips quirked.

"Useful? Are you a power tool?"

Some of the guys laughed. I'd already braced for the dig. Didn't care anymore.

I stared back at him until his amusement faded. He crushed the cigarette with an exhale that was neither disappointment nor anger—just a man releasing breath to replace the next, with the same cadence of a father removing his glasses before telling you to shut the fuck up and enjoy being young.

"Be a lawyer, Marcus." The advice sounded almost paternal, the tone of his voice momentarily shifting from the icy, paranoid inflection that accompanied street politics and vetting by way of gunpoint. But it was his smile—the kind that suggested this hadn't been anything but a joke to him from the beginning, a boredom-killing favor—that cemented the one glaring, irrefutable truth underlying this unsettling, monumentally awkward game of cartel jeopardy.

I *was* a child.

And 'idiot' didn't even begin to cover it.

"Sir, I—" I began, but was cut off by a sound that sliced through the room like a machete.

WHAM.

The group's eyes darted across the room as one. An enforcer dragged a beat-up captive, bound and hysterical, out from a closet where he'd apparently been stored like luggage this entire time. He kicked the man's legs apart and forced him into a kneel, subsequently cocking a handgun and sticking the barrel into his lacerated cheek. The captive whimpered fearfully, words escaping him in terrified gasps.

I watched all of this unfold in stunned horror, my body frozen in place, unable to look away from the human drama playing out with all the subtlety of a slaughterhouse. Conversely, Buddy seemed relatively nonplussed, as if the appearance of a man about to be executed was nothing more remarkable than a waiter bringing the check.

"What did he..." I began, but couldn't finish the question.

"I suggest you leave. Now." Santiago's voice was soft but carried the inevitability of gravity.

I nervously glanced at Buddy who responded with a silent nod of agreement. I stood up, feeling Alejandro's presence at my rear like a shadow with substance. Buddy gave Luis a hug, and we separated without another word.

As we were escorted out, I could hear the captive's desperate pleas fading behind us: "Please, *señor, yo no sabía, yo no sabía, yo no sabía—*"

I didn't know, I didn't know, I didn't know.

Santiago's response was equally clear: "SHUT UP! And *you.* What did I tell you about the fucking floor, *pendejo?*"

For the next year, I thought I'd escaped, that the brief intersection of my small-time operation with the genuine article had been just that—brief. I went back to my life and tried to forget the look in that kneeling man's eyes, the casual way Santiago had dismissed me, and the realization of just how deep the waters were that I'd been playing in.

Eventually, the smell of bleach, leather, and expensive tobacco in the Waldorf was replaced by the cloying scent of yeast, drip coffee, and industrial cinnamon as I traded the digital scale for a cash register at a UCLA bakery.

By 2016, I had forgotten about all of it. I deleted my list of numbers and laid low, convincing myself that selling on campus was a fever dream I'd finally woken up from.

My life became a series of harmless, lukewarm transactions. No one was kneeling in the walk-in fridge. No one was checking my father's DUIs. I was safe, boring, and utterly invisible. My grades were good. And so was I.

One morning, as I clipped order receipts above the counter, my phone vibrated. I reached for it and glanced at the lock screen, the message displayed there like a summons from another life.

13 Leon Ave., San Diego. 9 P.M. Package. Don't fuck up.

And just like that... I was back in it. Back on a path I thought I'd left behind, pulled by invisible strings I hadn't even known were attached to me. Whatever illusion of choice I'd been maintaining vanished like a match in rain.

The magician had revealed his trick, and I was it.

4

DEAD MAN WALKING

The address led to a low-income neighborhood, the kind you see driving out of San Diego and across the border. Not the San Diego they put on postcards, with its gleaming hotels and pristine beaches, but the forgotten, strung-out cousin no one invites to family gatherings, or the one they hide the paint from. Caged windows stared back at me like it was *my* fault, barbed wire fences guarding shacks of homes that seemed to sink into the dirt, like the earth was trying to swallow them out of mercy.

I stepped out of my car wearily. A German Shepherd whimpered at me from inside a chain-link fence, his eyes too intelligent for comfort. The animal looked at me like I was wearing a sign that said ABOUT TO MAKE TERRIBLE DECISIONS.

Dogs have that gift. Much like evil, they can spot stupidity from a mile away, probably because they spend their lives watching humans do inexplicably dumb shit like stick forks in electrical outlets and marry people they met on dating apps or in court-ordered rehab. After a few thousand years of watching us walk into traffic and not being able to say a goddamn word about it, the instinct must've just calcified into their DNA—a sixth sense for human idiocy, bred into the species like herding or the compulsion to eat their own vomit.

This particular German Shepherd had the expression of a parole officer played by Paul Walter Hauser reviewing my resume: disappointed but not surprised, concerned but not completely invested. I half-expected him to shake his head and get back to eating a Subway sandwich. Even the neighborhood wildlife knew I was fucked.

I crouched. Clicked my tongue.

"You okay, buddy?" A question more for myself.

SHOOM!

A blacked-out Challenger bulleted past me. The car slowed and braked into a garage a few houses down, the squeal of tires advertising its arrival to anyone within earshot. Four Hispanic men emerged, scanning the street with the learned vigilance of sentries.

I walked into the space, guarded but playing it cool—at least hoping I was. The four men looked at me with the car still running, Mexican radio providing a soundtrack of accordions and rapid-fire Spanish. One asked me something I couldn't understand, his tone somewhere between hostile and hostile.

"No hable, man," I responded, my pronunciation so terrible I offended myself.

A towering, bald Latino man with a handlebar mustache, angry-looking muscles, and more tattoos than I could mentally process leaned against the hood of the Challenger.

Javier Lopez. Who I would later come to learn was quite possibly the *worst* person I could've drawn on my first job. Javier ran reception from the border and distribution into the California mainland—the ugly, invisible work of moving product and people north through the corridor and fanning it out into the cities. Recruitment, logistics, enforcement. If you've ever wondered who handles the American end of the pipeline—who meets the mules, pays the kids, and buries the ones who talk—it was men like Javier. Grimy, violent, ruthless work, done primarily against his own people, which made him either a pragmatist or a monster depending on who you asked. Most people didn't ask.

"Who are you?" he asked. Valid.

"I got a text." *Dude—really?*

Javier straightened. "From who?"

I could feel every set of eyes on me like individual cigarette burns, each one finding a new spot to land.

"I met with some guy like a year ago at a hotel, Santiago or something..." I realized as I spoke that I was babbling. "I don't know—someone told me to come here."

"So you got a text, telling you to come *here*... and to say you know a Santiago?" His lips quirked with amusement. "What, you think all wetbacks know each other?"

His men chuckled. On cue, the garage door began to close behind me with a horrible scraping noise—and if you listened closely enough, it might've been laughing too.

I made a mental note to haunt the shit out of my community college counselor back in Philly, as this was definitely not the "true California experience" I'd been promised. Although, to be fair, getting murdered by strangers in shitty neighborhoods was pretty authentically California. I just thought it would at least happen in the back alley of a nightclub with Kavinsky or something playing in the background, not in a border-adjacent single-family garage that smelled like motor oil and sweat. Also, he probably hadn't factored in me swapping a 4.0 for an oil barrel.

Yep—on me.

"Look, I just drove from Los Angeles," I said, like that mattered. "I just need to know if I'm in the right place."

"The right place, you say?" He chuckled. "Santiago's dead, *amigo.*"

Well, shit.

"What are you talking about?"

Fuck, fuck, fuck, fuck.

"It's old news, really. OD'd on horse in East Hollywood. Would you like to try again?"

Santiago, my one connection to legitimacy in this underbelly, who hadn't even fucking *liked* me, had gone full-tilt "Carmelita" while I was selling scones to Asian kids.

"No, that's fine. I-I'll just go."

He frowned with genuine confusion. "Go where?"

Good question. Javier's men had fully boxed me in like a pack of salivating wolves circling wounded prey.

My shoulders dropped.

A goon attacked from behind. I sensed it more than saw it, some primal instinct for self-preservation kicking in about a two-hour drive too late, and swung around, catching him hard in the nose with a punch that surprised both of us.

I sprinted to the side door and pulled on the knob with desperate strength, but it might as well have been welded shut. His buddy came over and cracked me in the right shoulder blade with the butt of a snub-nose magnum, crumpling me to the concrete floor.

The third goon, who may have just wanted to be involved at this point, then helped drag me toward a ping-pong table, slamming the side of my head down on its surface and aiming the revolver at my temple.

I'd always wondered what my last thought would be. Turns out, as that cold metal kissed my skin with the tenderness of a restraining order, it was...

Fuck.

One of them grabbed a hammer, forcefully planting my right hand onto the table, preparing to deliver the kind of damage you don't recover from. I closed my eyes, waiting for the agony that would signal the end of my pitiful criminal career and possibly my life, when—

"Luis Reyes! Call Luis Reyes!" The words burst from me with the volume and desperation of a drowning man breaking the surface.

The mayhem halted.

"Luis Reyes. Of the Reyes Cartel. Go ahead, call him. He'll vouch for me if he hasn't already."

Javier looked at his men. Then he looked back at me, a loaded beat passing between us as he considered. He reached into his pocket and pulled out a Motorola from the Great Depression. His eyes darted between my smushed face and the dial-pad as he punched in numbers with menacing deliberation. The line was quickly picked up:

"Luis. *Sí.*"

The conversation continued in Spanish, peppered with occasional glances at me.

"Gringo? La coca?"

The words registered through my panic—they were talking about cocaine. Not weed. The realization landed like a brick in my gut, followed by the companion one that I was, in fact, a fucking idiot.

They talked a little bit more in rapid-fire Spanish. Javier laughed, more relaxed now. The goon that I'd rocked, still holding me down, leaned into my ear and delivered his own brand of a sweet nothing:

"You're fucked now, white boy."

I squirmed. Useless. Survival was impossible, only plausible in the event—

Javier hung up with a smile.

Almost a little disappointed, they separated from me, allowing me to rise to my feet.

"For the pick-up?" Javier asked, his tone suddenly professional, businesslike, even sunny.

I wiped blood from my lip with the back of my hand. "Yeah, that's what I was—"

"You probably should've opened with that," he smiled, all teeth and no warmth.

He patted me on the shoulder with faux camaraderie. Pointed to the Challenger.

"In the trunk."

Javier whistled. One of them unlatched the trunk with a practiced flick. I walked over and looked inside, the sight hitting me like another pistol to the shoulder blade: four dense, wrapped bricks of cocaine, pristine white packages wrapped in plastic and tape, each one a felony sentence waiting to happen.

"What's this?" The question was stupid, even adolescent, but shock has a way of making idiots of us all.

"You've never seen bricks before?"

"I thought I was picking up weed." The admission came out small, pathetic.

"Your keys," one of the goons demanded.

I looked at him. "What?"

"Your keys. To pull in." His breath was hot and reeked of Texaco or whatever donkey piss these people drank between kabob-ing families of four for some pear-shaped middle schooler in Arizona to watch on gore.net.

Mechanically, I handed him the keys. Behind me, Javier reached into a white fridge and pulled out two Modelos, snapping the heads off with a bottle opener that hung from his belt loop.

"You got fight in you. I respect that." He handed me a beer, foam spilling over its stocky neck. "Forgive my men. It's a border town."

"Right," I said, shakily sipping the beer that I didn't want but probably needed.

The goons began to load my trunk with the product. I watched, detached, like I was observing someone else's life unfold in a movie I hadn't chosen to watch. Somewhere between the first brick and the fourth, the German Shepherd from the fence started barking—loud, sustained, furious—as if trying, one last time, to talk some sense into me.

And so I became a mule, a courier of other people's poison. The drive back to Los Angeles was the longest of my life, every police car a potential end to my freedom, every pothole a reminder of the contraband in my trunk. I kept precisely at the speed limit, signaled every lane change, and held my breath whenever a patrol car appeared in my rearview. Two hours and forty-seven minutes of purgatory on the I-5, alone with the knowledge of what I was carrying and the increasingly obvious suspicion that I had crossed a line I couldn't uncross.

I made it back to LA in one piece. The delivery went smoothly, my role as middleman complete and my pockets about five thousand bucks droopier.

But I didn't stay a mule for long. Buddy saw to that. Within a week, he'd gotten on the phone with Luis and made the case that I was wasted on transport, that a kid who could talk his way into frat houses, dorm rooms, and faculty parties at UCLA could do the same thing on Sunset Boulevard, just with better margins. Luis, to his credit or discredit, agreed. I was given carte blanche to build my own book of business, answering only to Luis through Buddy, with the kind of operational freedom that should've terrified me but instead felt like a promotion.

So I quit school without a backward glance like the overzealous, ungrateful little shit I was and bought an off-market two-bedroom apartment in West Hollywood through a friend of Luis'. Cash deal. Almost immediately, I installed a safe—Smith & Wesson Depository, fourteen-by-sixteen—in the walk-in closet and began my new life as something more than a college dealer but less than a career criminal—or so I told myself.

And I was good at it. The same instincts I'd sharpened moving product to my peers—reading a room, knowing who was holding back and who was ready to spend, calibrating exactly how much friendliness a transaction required—translated seamlessly to a wealthier clientele. The hustle was identical; only the tax brackets changed.

I began cultivating a master list with the discipline of a stockbroker building a Rolodex: names, preferences, schedules, habits, vices. Who liked to party on Thursdays. Who needed delivery to a back entrance. Who paid cash and who needed to be reminded. Turns out, the gap between a nineteen-year-old sorority girl and a thirty-five-year-old television producer was a lot narrower than either would've liked to admit. Their trust came cheap, and their attention even cheaper. All you had to do was show up on time with what they wanted and pretend you didn't notice how badly they needed it.

Buddy's family knew people in high places: producers, directors, stars whose faces adorned billboards and magazine covers. From Laurel Canyon to the Hollywood Hills, I made drops, handing off baggies, white and green, to important-looking people in front of important-looking houses. I became efficient, habitual, a ghost moving through the margins of Los Angeles. I did my best to fit in among the beautiful and damned, mimicking the easy confidence of someone who belonged in these rarefied circles.

Usually, I'd be in and out, the transaction clean and mostly impersonal. But then I stayed once, accepting an invitation to linger, and before I knew it, I was smoking a joint poolside with some dried-up former child stars I used to watch on Nickelodeon. And they all just wanted drugs, it was *surreal*—these successful people, these role models, as hungry for escape as any Pico Boulevard junkie.

Off white alone, Buddy and I were drawing in north of a grand per night. But I wasn't pushing anything bigger than eight-balls. I had about twenty regular clients. Producers, actors, writers, directors, DJs. Their notability varied but what they all had in common was *money*, and too much time on their hands.

Hell, even a certain blonde pop singer was a client until she wrapped her Porsche around a pole on Rodeo Drive after an all-night bender that I'd supplied the fuel for. But that's a story for another day. And it should go without saying, but if you were calling a minute before eight or a minute after eleven...

Well, fuck you.

Even drug dealers need boundaries, some separation between the person they are and the service they provide.

Oh, and I got a piece 'cause, anybody in the game will tell you, you gotta have a piece. A sleek .45 that I practiced with at ranges far from my regular haunts, developing the kind of accuracy you hope you never need to use.

Buddy liked to go out and celebrate our success, throwing money around like confetti. Whatever we'd drop on a night out, he'd make sure we doubled the following week. We'd hit clubs where the cover charge cost more than my father's weekly paycheck back in Philly, drink bottles that cost what I used to make in a month serving cinnamon rolls. I watched him throw money around like it was nothing, because to him, it was.

I was learning the business from the inside out, but each transaction, each brick moved, each wad of cash counted and hidden were stones placed in a path leading somewhere I couldn't yet see, but should have feared. The irony wasn't lost on me, even then: I'd come to LA to become somebody, and had instead become a ghost, a shadow, a facilitator of other people's escapes while creating a prison for myself.

In other words, a dead man walking.

5

THE MAN IN BLACK

One of my clients was a washed-up former sitcom star who'd stooped to teaching "acting classes" in a rundown black box theater in WeHo. It was mostly a scam, a way for the old asshole to get laid. The guy was like a walking PSA for why the #MeToo movement needed to exist. He'd shuffle around the studio in flip-flops that had seen better decades and more honest casting couches, his Costco readers teetering perilously at the tip of his defunct nose. He used to name-drop that he grew up Episcopalian, like that was supposed to mean something. Probably thought it made him sound less predatory. All it meant was he fucked with the lights on and said sorry after. His acting resume peaked sometime during the Reagan administration, but he carried himself like he was still getting residual checks instead of restraining orders. The sad part? It worked. Los Angeles was full of girls who'd trade dignity for the illusion of industry connection, who'd convinced themselves that letting some washed-up sitcom nobody cop a feel was just "paying dues." I sold him coke twice a week at a horrendous mark-up—probably the only thing keeping his dick hard for whatever insecure Poli-Sci major from Northridge he pretended was promising.

But it *did* catch the attention of the starry-eyed strivers of LA, the ones not yet broken by rejection but already damaged enough to think this piece of shit's approval might matter. And one of them caught my eye, too.

Among the schmoozing students one evening, I saw a pretty girl with light skin and wavy black hair that caught the late afternoon sun streaming through the dirty windows. She was chatting with a friend, her laugh genuine in a way that stood out in this city of practiced emotions.

Simultaneously, a client I'd picked up residually and regretfully, who we'll call Squirrely Guy—balding but trying to hide it under a beanie, his paunch straining against a vintage T-shirt meant for someone twenty pounds lighter or twenty years younger—approached me in what he must have thought was a surreptitious way. I'd already clocked the smell of Del Taco and coconut foot spray before he'd even decided whether to stick his hands in his pockets, and I'd begun calculating where my patience reserves stood for the day before pretending to give a shit why he needed ecstasy—*more* of it, considering the only thing he was going home to after ruining his scene partner's one night of respite from tending a Northridge tiki bar was a chihuahua with Parkinson's and a roommate who I was pretty sure was a serial killer. None of that was a joke, just to clarify.

Three, two, *one*—

"Hey, man, you sell dick pills? Cialis? My doc won't refill my prescription again and—"

Yeah, fuck no. I moved past him without even a glance, catching up with the luminous stranger just before she was about to head off. We locked eyes, and something passed between us: a current of recognition, though we'd never met, or at least I certainly hoped we hadn't. I outstretched my hand, the gesture almost formal in its deliberateness.

"I'm Marcus."

"Stephanie," she said as she shook my hand. Her grip was firm, her palm cool and dry against mine. "I didn't see you in class..."

"Oh, I haven't, uh... officially signed up yet. Is it worth it?" I asked, feigning innocence.

"Well, if you were a girl, I'd tell you to stay out of arm's reach of that creeper. But I'm sure you'd do just fine." Her smile had an edge to it. I'd seen it before in the smarter girls who worked the clubs, the ones who could spot a producer's son from across a crowded room and calculate exactly how much attention was worth giving him.

But Stephanie wore it differently, like armor that hadn't yet become her skin. She was still soft underneath, still had that thing that made you want to protect her even when she clearly didn't need protecting.

"Thanks for the vote of confidence. You know, you look like you'd be a good actress." The line was transparent, but I delivered it with enough charm to make it land.

"Actor. We don't distinguish gender anymore like that." She corrected me with the patience of someone who'd done it many times before. "And what does a 'good actor' look like?"

"Confident. Composed. Like you." I wasn't lying—there was something in her carriage, in the directness of her gaze, that suggested a person comfortable in her own skin. A rarity in this city of reinvention.

"Good answer." Her smile softened into something more genuine.

I smiled back, feeling suddenly sheepish, almost boyish: a sensation I hadn't experienced in longer than I cared to admit. In that moment, with afternoon light painting her face in gold and shadow, I felt like I was meeting someone who might matter.

Which was dangerous as fuck, obviously. Nothing derails a criminal enterprise quite like catching feelings for a civilian. It was like being a vampire and falling for someone with a particularly nice clavicle: technically possible, but bound to end in either literal or proverbial arterial spray. The smart play would've been to get her number, never call it, and stick to new-age starlets who were already sociopaths in their own right. But I'd built my entire LA experience on a foundation of spectacularly poor decision-making, so why stop now? Besides, when was the last time I'd met someone who laughed like that? Someone who made me remember what it felt like to be a person instead of just a walking felony with a quota?

Later, we sat in a vinyl booth at Mel's Diner, the kind of place that trades on nostalgia for a time neither of us had lived through. Stephanie had ordered pancakes at 9 P.M., the childhood comfort food a small rebellion against adult conventions. I liked that about her immediately.

"So, what, you're from LA?" she asked, drowning her stack in syrup.

"Philly. I'm here for school." Combining a volunteered truth with the preservational lie. *Thanks, Dad.*

"What are you studying?"

"Pre-law." Another lie, though it had once been true.

"Oh, wow. You want to be a lawyer? Red flag." Her eyes crinkled at the corners as she grinned, softening the jab. "Just messing with you. Do you like it?"

I shrugged, evasive, unwilling to elaborate on a path I'd already abandoned.

"So, you from here?" I asked, redirecting.

"I am. Riverside, if you know where that is. But my parents moved out to Hermosa. Well, my mom did."

"They split?" I asked, recognizing the shadow that had fallen over face.

Stephanie nodded.

"Same," I offered, a small bridge between us.

"How old were you?"

"Not old enough." The answer was honest, stripped of pretense.

She nodded sweetly, a silent acknowledgment of shared experience. She got it—the way childhood ends not all at once but in stages, each parental failing another piece of innocence chipped away.

"Where'd your dad move?"

"Unless you consider rehab a place of residence, nowhere." The words had a practiced casualness, but I could hear the carefully banked pain beneath them.

"I'm sorry." The platitude was inadequate, but sincere.

"I was little. After his brother died, things went a little too far south for my mom's comfort." Her fingernail traced patterns in the condensation on her water glass, creating temporary art that vanished even as she made it.

"Drinker?" I asked, thinking of my own father, of whiskey bottles hidden behind bread.

"More of an opioid enthusiast." Her smile was wry, the humor a shield against deeper hurt.

I decided to let that breathe for a beat, respecting the boundaries around her pain. We all have our defenses, our ways of keeping the world at arm's length. I recognized hers because they mirrored my own.

"Well, I've never been to Hermosa," I said, changing the subject with deliberate lightness.

"It's this little beachfront town. Just past Manhattan."

"Huh?"

"The beach." Her laugh was gentle, instructive rather than mocking. "Manhattan Beach."

"Never been there, either."

"Do you like the beach? Generally?"

"You know, I like the water, it's just... all the sand." I gestured vaguely, searching for words. "Gets everywhere. In your shoes, your clothes. Your ass."

Stephanie laughed at that, the sound rich and unguarded.

"I'm serious," I continued, encouraged. "It drives me nuts."

"So beaches are off limits?" She raised an eyebrow, challenging.

I smiled. "I might be willing to give it another shot."

Later that night, we burst into my apartment, a tangle of limbs and lips and urgent hands. The door slammed behind us with the finality of a decision made, though neither of us had spoken it aloud.

"This is a nice place," she remarked between kisses, taking in the expensive minimalism that surrounded us.

I mumbled something noncommittal against her neck, my hands already working at the buttons of her blouse. We fell onto my couch, a black leather affair that had cost more than my first car. My dog, a pit bull named Rocco, watched us with bemused curiosity, his tongue lolling out in what looked suspiciously like judgment.

"Aw, you have a dog?" Stephanie paused, distracted by Rocco's soulful eyes.

"Yeah, that's Rocco." I tried to recapture her attention, my lips finding the sensitive spot below her ear.

"Hi, Rocco," she cooed, before turning back to me, our mouths meeting with renewed urgency.

Rocco had better taste in women than I did, which wasn't saying much since he once tried to hump a fire hydrant for twenty minutes. But he was giving Stephanie the look he usually reserved for the mailman: part curiosity, part assessment, like he was trying to figure out if she belonged in our little illicit ecosystem. Maybe he recognized something I was too fucked up to see clearly: that she was the first real thing to walk into this apartment.

We went back to kissing, to discovering each other's bodies with the mixed urgency and tentativeness of new lovers. There was something different about her: a presence, a groundedness that made me feel simultaneously more aware of myself and less alone. It was dangerous, that feeling. It made me want things I couldn't afford to want.

On another night, Stephanie and I walked through a movie theater lobby to our showing, snacks in hand. The smell of artificial butter and expectations hung in the air.

"Movie theater popcorn might be the biggest scam of our time," I said, looking at the overpriced bucket in my hands. "I mean, they buy it for thirty-three cents a sack, right? Then they turn around and stamp an eight-dollar price tag on it. It's criminal."

"But nothing beats that fake butter." She grinned, deliberately squirting more of the yellow substance onto her portion.

My pocket started vibrating, an unwelcome intrusion from the world I was trying to keep separate from these moments with her. I dug out my phone and glanced at the contact. It said *Mr. Reyes*. My stomach tightened, a Pavlovian response to the name that had come to represent obligation and danger in equal measure.

I stared at the screen for a moment as Stephanie continued, oblivious to the shift in my attention: "Besides, it's how they make their money, right? Like Dodger stadium. They practically give away the tickets and make it all back on seven-dollar hot dogs and nine-dollar beers."

I hit the forward button, rolling the dice on consequences I couldn't yet imagine.

In the theater, the film played, some forgettable action movie with explosions timed to cover plot holes, but I couldn't focus. My mind was elsewhere, calculating risks, imagining scenarios, planning exits. I was visibly restless, my knee bouncing, fingers drumming against the armrest. I leaned over to Stephanie, whispered something about needing the bathroom, and escaped into the relative sanity of the corridor.

As I exited, I didn't notice a man in all-black seated in a higher row, his eyes following my retreat.

In the bathroom, I splashed cold water on my face, trying to wash away the anxiety that clung to me like a second skin. The door opened behind me, and the man from the theater walked in, his movements deliberate and unhurried as he took position at the sink beside mine.

"'We shall not cease from exploration, and the end of all our exploring will be to arrive where we started and know the place for the first time,'" he said, his voice cultured, almost musical.

"What is that, Hawthorne?" I asked, feigning casual interest while my heart kicked against my ribs.

"TS Eliot." He corrected me without condescension, just simple fact.

"Not bad." I dried my hands with a paper towel, deliberately taking my time. "Do I know you?"

"Marcus, right? I've heard a lot about you." His smile was pleasant, professional. "And your girl... Stephanie. She's cute. I might've picked a better film, though."

My blood turned to ice water, the casual mention of her name a threat wrapped in pleasantry. "Okay..." I chuckled, the sound forced and brittle. "You know, I gotta say, you've really set the bar. For a hired gun, that is. You buy popcorn, too? An Icee? No, wait, let me guess: Blue Ras', right? I'm a Cherry man myself—"

"Don't flatter yourself. In this instance, I'm merely a messenger." His amusement seemed genuine, as if he found my bravado charming. "See, Diego Reyes is a busy man. He doesn't appreciate being forwarded by his handlers."

"Dude, I was just—" I started, scrambling for an excuse.

"There's a shipment coming in tomorrow. Oceanside." He cut me off, all business now.

"But I haven't even—"

"I wouldn't miss it. Remember, Marcus. A man is only as good as his principles. See you around, kid. Answer your phone."

The Man in Black tossed his balled-up paper towel into the garbage and exited without another word, leaving me frozen in place, my reflection in the mirror showing a face I barely recognized: pale, wide-eyed, the mask of confidence slipping to reveal the fear beneath.

What the fuck just happened? How did he know about Stephanie? How had he found me here, tonight, in this specific theater? The implications crawled over my skin like ants. I wasn't just being watched; I was being monitored. My life wasn't my own.

Frustration and helplessness coalesced into sudden rage. I muttered an expletive under my breath and kicked a trash can, the metallic clang echoing off the tiled walls. The violent action brought no relief, just a dull pain in my foot and the shameful awareness of my own impotence.

I stood there, breathing hard, staring at nothing, while around me the world continued its indifferent spin. Somewhere in the theater, Stephanie was waiting for me, wondering what was taking so long. She existed in a different reality from the one I'd just experienced: a normal world of movies and popcorn and simple pleasures.

I wanted that world. I wanted her world. But I was beginning to understand that it might not be mine to claim. The bathroom mirror reflected something wearing my face: a hollow-eyed, clueless piece of shit who'd traded Marcus Graves's soul for Diego Reyes' table scraps. How do you explain to someone like Stephanie that the nice apartment was a money-laundering operation? That the casual dinners were funded by human misery measured in kilos? That every time she laughed at my jokes, she was falling for a ghost, some idealized version of who I used to be before I became a professional destroyer of lives?

You can't. You just keep building the house of cards, knowing every kiss is borrowed time, every tender moment is stolen from the grave I'm digging for both of us. Because that's what guys like me do: we find something pure and we contaminate it. We take girls who still believe in happy endings and we drag them into our noir bullshit until they're just another casualty before discarding under the justification of necessity. The worst part, though? I knew exactly what I was doing. I wasn't some naive kid stumbling into trouble. I was the latter.

I was an apex predator draped in a passable skin suit, and Stephanie was just the latest victim of a pathological need to matter to someone who didn't know better.

6

2017

In 2017, everything changed.

On a cool Thursday night, Buddy and I walked into a pulsating nightclub on Sunset with bass heavy enough to rearrange my internal organs. The bouncer, a mountain of a man with neck tattoos and hands like cinder blocks, quickly waved us past the line of hopefuls shivering in clothes too revealing for the evening chill.

"Mr. Graves," he grinned, unhooking the velvet rope. "Good to see you."

I slipped him a folded hundred-dollar bill and kept walking, the gesture automatic now, part of the unspoken choreography of my weeknights. Money as lubricant, easing every transaction, smoothing every interaction.

It was embarrassing how quickly I'd adapted to this particular form of corruption. Six months ago, I would've agonized over spending a hundred dollars on groceries. Now I was casually bribing bouncers like some trust-fund asshole whose biggest problem was deciding which Lamborghini to drive to Erewhon.

"Where's my affirmation?" Buddy asked once we were inside, his tone mock-hurt but with an undertone of genuine complaint.

"I'm the field agent, aren't I?"

"Whatever. I got some people for you to meet."

We made our way to a cordoned-off area where a plastered Luis Reyes held court with a bald Armenian man I didn't recognize. Luis's eyes were bloodshot, his movements just a beat too slow—the look of someone who'd been celebrating for hours and had no intention of stopping.

"Happy birthday, boss." I shook Luis's hand diplomatically, the appropriate deference in my grip.

"Thank you, my friend," he slurred, his smile too wide.

Luis poured four shots and gleefully distributed them. Around that moment, I glanced across the bar and locked eyes with a woman—twenties, black hair—smiling in my direction, her gaze a hook I could physically feel. Luis tapped my arm, distracting me from the silent invitation.

"To success," Luis declared, raising his glass.

We all repeated the toast and slammed them back, the tequila burning a path down my throat—top shelf, as promised, but still fire. I set the glass down and found myself looking again for the woman who'd been watching me, but Luis redirected my attention once more.

"Have you met my friend?" He gestured to the bald man beside him. I had not. "Owner of the second-largest jewelry store in Beverly Hills. He'll fix you up nice, for a price."

"Pleasure. Marcus." I shook the man's hand, quickly registering the Rolex on his wrist.

"Simon Gideon," he introduced himself, his eyes flicking briefly to my bare wrist. "Looks like you need a watch."

"You think so?" I asked, amused by the immediate sales pitch.

Before Simon could answer, a new presence darkened our orbit: a statue of a man fitted into an all-black suit, with two similar figures hovering at his flanks. Don Silva, Mexican but with the bearing of European aristocracy, approached our group with the confident stride of someone who never questioned his welcome. When he moved, it was with the practiced grace of someone who'd learned that wasted motion could mean the difference between prosperity and dismemberment. His suit was tailored to perfection, but I noticed how it hung just right to conceal whatever hardware he was carrying.

"Ah, *cabrón*..." Buddy muttered under his breath, the tension in his body immediate and telling.

"Luis, Buddy. Pleasure as always." Don's voice was smooth, cultured, with just enough accent to remind you of his origins.

"Don!" Luis's greeting was just a shade too enthusiastic to be genuine. "You've met my friends, yes?"

Don's eyes slid over Simon dismissively before landing on me with an uncanny focus. "All but the prodigy."

There's a particular way killers look at each other—not with the theatrical menace you see in movies, but with the quiet assessment of any kind of professional. Don Silva had that look, the same one I'd seen in Santiago's eyes at the Waldorf, the same one I practiced in mirrors when I thought nobody was watching. It was the gaze of someone calculating value—threat level, usefulness, expendability. I'd been on the receiving end enough times to recognize it, but this was different. This time, I could feel myself looking back the same way without even meaning to, and that realization was infinitely more unsettling than his scrutiny.

"Marcus, Don, Don, Marcus." Luis performed the introduction with forced casualness.

Don and I shook hands, his grip firm but not aggressive.

"You two are making quite the name for yourselves," he said, a statement that could be compliment, insult, or threat.

"Just seeing our end," I replied noncommittally, a phrase vague enough to mean everything or nothing.

"Whatever you're doing, keep it up." Don patted my back, the gesture friendly but the pressure just a little too firm, the placement a little too close to my neck.

I immediately tensed.

Don then proceeded to wrap his right arm around Luis like some sort of annoying older cousin: "I remember the first time I met this slippery son of a bitch. It was a party of his on the roof of a Four Seasons in San Diego. He was so drunk, he could barely stand. *El pinche pendejo* was pissing off the railing! He would've fallen sixteen stories, but I saved him. Since then, I've encouraged him to stay grounded."

"*Chinga tu madre,*" Luis responded, the words just slightly—only slightly—lacking the humor they were meant to convey.

"But life should not only be lived, it should be celebrated. And with that, my friend, I say to you: happy birthday." Don's smile was cinema-perfect, the kind that never reached his eyes, which were flat and calculating as a reptile's. I'd seen that exact expression before in old newspaper photos of cartel bosses at charity galas, their arms around local politicians who'd be found in car trunks three months later. Don had perfected the art of *looking* friendly while mentally sizing you up for a body bag. "Give Diego my regards."

Luis just nodded and shrugged off Don's arm.

"Well, I should be off. Gentlemen." Don straightened his jacket, a dismissal disguised as a departure.

I followed Don with my eyes as he rallied his men and split, something about his presence lingering like cigar smoke even after he'd gone. What bothered me most wasn't what Don had said—it was what he *hadn't*. The way he'd cataloged every face in our group, filing away names and relationships for future reference. How his bodyguards had positioned themselves to watch exits, not entrances. Most unsettling was the proprietary way he'd touched Luis, like a farmer checking livestock before slaughter. Everything about the interaction felt like an inspection, a final assessment before some predetermined action.

On top of it all, it reminded me of something ol' Barbara Graves told me once: *"When someone greets hospitality with condescension, that's all you need to see."*

Buddy leaned into my ear, his breath hot and tequila-scented: "Guy's a grade-A prick. Walks around like a king when he's really a bishop. Don't let him bother you. Let's get a drink, man."

I remained frozen, still watching Don and his men until they fully vanished into the crowd, something about his manner triggering warning bells I couldn't quite place.

"Marcus," Buddy prompted, impatient now.

"Right," I said, snapping out of it. "Right, let's get a drink."

My phone started buzzing in my pocket, the familiar vibration pattern that meant one thing: Stephanie. Buddy rolled his eyes, already knowing who it was without seeing the screen.

"Shit. One second." I gestured a frantic apology and stepped aside, plugging my ear with a finger like I was trying to manual-reset my own brain. I hit *Accept* and screamed into the receiver:

"HEY, BABE! I'M JUST OUT WITH BUDDY! WHAT'S UP?!"

The words didn't just leave my mouth; they felt like they were being fired out of a cannon. To Stephanie, I probably sounded like a man being kidnapped by a very enthusiastic marching band.

"Did you drive?" Stephanie's voice was tinny and distant.

"NO, WE UBERED!" I bellowed, the lie sliding out with the practiced ease of a professional con artist. "UBER! LIKE THE APP, STEPH!"

Lying to her had become as natural as breathing, which should have bothered me more than it did. Each deception built on the last, creating an elaborate mythology where Marcus Graves was still a law student with normal problems—student loans, midterms, whether to cook or starve. She lived in that fiction, and I was its author, carefully crafting a character she could love while the real me dissolved in cocaine residue and cartel blood money.

"Why are you talking so loud?"

"IT'S THE MUSIC!" I pivoted away from a group of dancing women, trying to find a pocket of air that didn't vibrate at the frequency of a tectonic plate shift. "IT'S NUTS IN HERE! WHAT?"

"Anybody performing?" Her question was casual, but I sensed the undercurrent: the silent GPS ping of a girlfriend checking the perimeter.

"NO, IT'S—" I started, but the words died in my throat.

Someone had materialized beside me. It was the girl from earlier, close enough that her perfume cut through the smell of sweat and expensive gin like a silver blade. I froze as I met her eyes.

"What?" Stephanie prompted from the other end of the line, her voice now a suspicious needle in my ear.

"NO, IT'S JUST A REGULAR NIGHT!" I finished, my volume dropping slightly as the adrenaline of being caught spiked. "LOOK, I'LL CALL YOU WHEN I GET HOME! LOVE YOU! BYE!"

"Girlfriend?" the woman asked, her voice a perfect mix of husky and sweet, like honey over gravel.

"What do you care?" I countered, unexpectedly hostile.

"What's your name?" She was unfazed by my rudeness, a small smile playing at the corners of her lips.

"What's yours?" I deflected again, playing for time as I tried to place her. She looked vaguely familiar, but in LA, everyone does. This city manufactures a certain type of beauty with the formulaic discipline of an assembly line.

"Asked you first."

I studied her for a moment, caution warring with interest. "Marcus."

"I'm Roxy," she offered, extending a hand with long, manicured nails painted a deep burgundy.

"Nice to meet you, Roxy." I shook her hand briefly, noting the firmness of her grip, the deliberate way her fingers lingered against mine.

"Wanna do some coke?"

"I don't have any."

"That's not what I asked." Her eyes held mine, challenging and inviting at once.

I hesitated, the responsible part of my brain—the part that thought about Stephanie, about consequences, about the fine line I was already walking—briefly winning out. But then that part seceded, as it always seemed to when temptation presented itself with enough force.

"Lead the way," I heard myself say, and followed her through the crowd toward the bathrooms, already calculating how I'd justify this to myself later.

See, the thing about moral compromise is that it's like any other addiction: the first hit makes you sick, but by the hundredth, you're just trying to feel normal. Following Roxy toward whatever chemical oblivion she was offering felt fated, not because I wanted the drugs, but because I'd trained myself to say "yes" to every temptation that crossed my path. Each transgression made the next one easier, each boundary crossed made the next one seem arbitrary.

I wasn't falling anymore. I was diving, eyes wide open, into whichever abyss would have me.

7

MARK HIS GRAVE

Diego Reyes' death created a power vacuum that nature couldn't tolerate.

The transfer of power was swift, with Don Silva assuming control of the Reyes cartel. For me and Buddy, the months that followed were business as usual on the surface. But currents were shifting. It was like living in a house with a cracked foundation: everything looked normal until you noticed the subtle warping of door frames, the way glasses slid across tables that weren't quite level anymore.

Most notably, Buddy's behavior had shifted from sporadic self-destruction to outright recklessness. Late. Nodding off. Fighting clients. There's grief, and then there's dousing your entire life in gasoline just to see if the spark of your pain is hot enough to light it. With every bender and black-eyed declaration of apathy, he drifted further out to sea, leaving me with the gnawing realization that it wouldn't be him that became stranded, but me.

It was 2019.

I sat in Dr. Christopher Mann's office, the psychiatrist's cool eyes regarding me with professional detachment. He wore a blue-collar shirt with horn-rimmed glasses.

"You and Stephanie... Have you stayed in touch?" he asked.

"We have, actually. I guess I thought it'd be weirder."

"How so?"

"Well... with how it ended, you know? I felt terrible. Like, *really* bad." The memory of her finding me with Roxy in my apartment still made my stomach clench with guilt. Some memories don't fade; they just get quieter, like a dog that stops barking but never stops watching the door.

"That's understandable."

"Then why'd I do it?"

"Why does any young man generally do as he pleases?" Dr. Mann countered.

I gave that one a moment. "Because he thinks he'll get away with it?"

"You tell me."

"I thought that's why I was here. So you could give me the answers."

"If only it were that simple. I *can* speak from experience, though." He adjusted his glasses thoughtfully. "Typically, when I see people make self-destructive choices, they're doing so because, on some level, they feel they're undeserving of what they have in life. So, consciously or otherwise, they aim to strip themselves of that which they feel they haven't earned."

The room got smaller. Not literally, but in the way rooms do when someone says something you've spent years not saying to yourself.

"Like... imposter syndrome?"

"I prefer 'bullshit.'"

I smiled. First real one in weeks. "Can I ask you something?"

"Why on earth would you do that?" he joked.

"Is it wrong to do bad things out of love?"

He considered this carefully. "It depends on whether or not you're deluding yourself. Are you really doing these things for others, or are you using them as a convenient shield to mask actions undertaken out of pure ego? If it's the latter, love doesn't figure into that equation."

His alarm went off before I could respond.

"Sorry about that." He turned it off. "That was quite a substantial session, Marcus. I'd love to expand on it."

I stood, pulling out a prewritten check from my pocket. "Expand on what?"

"You."

"I appreciate that, Dr. Mann. But I'm pretty busy." I handed him the slip of paper, already retreating behind my usual defenses.

"Clearly something told you that you needed this hour. If the urge strikes you for another, I'd hope to be the first to know."

"You think anybody else would take me?" I joked, and turned for the door. "Take care, Dr. Mann. How 'bout them Eagles this Thursday?"

He scoffed. "Not a worry in the world, my friend."

I left.

***

That night, I attended a party in the Hollywood Hills, where drugs flowed like water and everyone pretended to be someone better than themselves. As I prepared to leave, the owner, Sam Griffith (also known as DJ Wilcox), caught me by the door.

"Sam. Pleasure as always."

"Pleasure's mine. Just keep bringing the heat, my boy. You bouncing?" His pupils were blown wide.

"I should crash."

"Dropping by Saturday? Same shit, you in?"

"I'll see," I called over my shoulder, already halfway out the door.

Driving through Beverly Hills afterward, I spoke to Stephanie hands-free.

"You asked me what I did tonight and I told you: work," I said, defensive before she'd even accused me of anything.

"In the Hollywood Hills? Just because I'm still talking to you doesn't mean I'm a complete idiot." She paused. "Or maybe it does."

"Give me a break. It was this engineering guy I had to meet with. Computer dude. Built his own company. Lots of great insight."

Not my best.

"You're still taking those classes, right?"

"Tuesdays and Thursdays," I replied with faux enthusiasm.

"How's your mom?"

"Fuck if I know."

"You should call her."

"Yep."

"I'm serious, Marcus. Why do you avoid your family? It's not healthy."

"You're right."

"I usually am." She was.

"Why'd we break up again?"

"Because you're an asshole." I was.

I got another call—my neighbor Josh. "One sec'. I'll call you back."

I switched over. "Yo."

"Marcus?"

"What's going on, Josh?"

"You home?"

"Beverly Hills. Should be getting in soon. Why?"

"You got a girl waiting for you or something?"

"What?" Alarm bells rang in my head.

"It's... Something's moving around next door."

"Moving around? How?" My hand tightened on the steering wheel.

"Like, little thuds. Walking around and shit."

"Probably just Rocco being restless. Couldn't walk him this morning."

"That's what I figured."

"You see anybody?"

"Didn't look."

"Do me a favor and take a little peek into the hallway, will you?"

"You got it."

"Thanks, man. Appreciate it."

I switched back to Stephanie, trying to keep the tension from my voice. "Hey, are you at my place?"

"Uh, no. I'm in Hermosa, Marcus. With my mom. Remember I told you?"

"Right. That's what I thought."

"What's going on?"

"Neighbor said he was hearing something. I don't know."

Josh called back. "Uh, good night, Steph. Talk tomorrow."

"Good night," she replied, and hung up.

"Anything?" I asked Josh immediately.

"Nada."

"Lock your door."

"Way ahead of you, buddy."

I hung up and accelerated.

When I reached my apartment building, I moved cautiously down the hallway, every sense heightened. Entering my unit, I withdrew a switchblade, popping it open. I rounded the corner with the blade at waist-level, only to find Rocco waiting with a toy in his mouth.

Still, I checked my safe. Naturally, the neatly-piled money, the .45, and the ounce of coke were all present and accounted for.

In the guest bedroom, I found my father, William Graves, in his usual state—balding, decrepit, snoring in a wheelchair. SportsCenter droned on a miniature monitor in front of him. I'd moved him in after his Medicaid ran out, another responsibility I bore with complicated emotions. There's something particularly fucked up about having your alcoholic father drooling and withering away in your guest bedroom while you count cartel money in the next room.

I shut off the TV and lights before exiting.

Back in the kitchen, I reached into the fridge for a beer.

Then I spotted something out of place.

A separate bottle cap, freshly cracked and lying on the counter.

My phone vibrated.

I answered.

"Hello."

"Hey, can you come to my place? We need to talk."

Buddy.

Tense.

***

I drove to his apartment building, the night air carrying a chill that seemed to seep into my bones.

As I walked down the corridor to his unit, memories from earlier flashed through my mind: a bathroom in Sam Griffith's house, me puking after one line too many. I'd called Buddy from there.

"These girls are crazy, man. I don't know what they're putting in the food these days," I'd said, trying to sound casual.

"Me neither, but I'm not complaining," he replied.

"Anyway, you're not gonna get in better with these people if you don't try to pretend a little bit."

"Why would I want to pretend?"

"It's cool. I'm going home anyway."

"Word."

"Hey, how are those keys I gave you? I can pick them up in the morning now that my dad's set up."

"Gone."

"Already? That's impressive. You just used my list, right?"

He had paused then.

"Yup," he finally said, "just the names on it."

"You're the man."

The exchange echoed in my head as I opened the door to Buddy's apartment. I walked slowly into the living room...

And found Buddy planted on the couch, glassy-eyed and bleeding from his hairline.

"The fuck?"

THWACK! Something hard connected with the back of my head, dropping me to my knees with an aluminum vibration I felt in my tonsils. Through blurred vision, I saw an enforcer circle into view, a chrome slugger in his hands. The Man in Black from the movie theater was also present, watching impassively.

I looked at Buddy, who stared back with tears in his eyes.

"I'm sorry, Marcus."

"What is this, man?" I said, still stunned.

Don Silva walked into the room.

"Something that could've been avoided."

"What the fuck are you doing here?"

"You never struck me as somebody who needed things spelled out, Marcus."

I looked to Buddy, who was still semi-despondent.

"What happened, dude?"

"I'm really, really sorry," he said, voice cracking.

"Stop fucking saying that! You're freaking me out! What happened?"

"I really fucked up."

Don took a seat. "Marcus, do you know how much seven kilos of cocaine is worth?"

"For our shit? North of one-fifty on any given day. Who gives a fuck?"

"One-sixty-eight," Buddy corrected automatically.

"Thank you, Buddy." Don found my eyes again. "Lots of money, right?"

"*Yeah*, lots of money," I mocked back, all Anglo snark, like I wasn't kneeling on a tarp in Hell's waiting room. "Why?"

Don didn't answer, just wore that infuriating smile and waited. And just like that, piece... met piece... met... piece.

Oh.

"No..." I heard myself whisper, denial flooding to soothe the initial onset of horror.

"I'm an idiot," Buddy said.

"What the fuck did you do?"

"I went on a bender. Started with an eight-ball at the club, and... I went *crazy*, man. And you weren't—"

"I wasn't what?! I was *busy*, you asshole!"

"Yes, he told us," Don interjected. "Your father, cancer. Heart-breaking."

I ignored him, focused entirely on Buddy. "I thought maybe I could trust you after four fucking years!"

"I didn't do all of it. But I was carrying it in the car. Cops have been sniffing around my place. I got paranoid." Buddy's words tumbled out. "One night, I went to this strip club. Garden of Eden. I forgot I had it."

I buried my face in my hands.

"I don't know if the trunk was unlocked, or... if people heard—"

"*Heard?* Who the fuck did you tell?!"

"I might've told some of the girls about it. Trying to get them to come home with me. I was wasted, man. And when I got back to the car, it was all gone."

"You didn't go back in?"

"I tried."

"Who runs it?"

"The Arab dude—you know him."

Don checked his watch. "You two done? I'd like to get back to my children."

I glanced at the ground, noticing for the first time that it was covered in plastic sheeting. Buddy started crying like a little kid.

It was the most horrifying thing I'd ever heard.

I tried to shift gears.

"Where's your cousin?"

"Buddy will be joining him momentarily," Don said, which is when I noticed the gun in his hands.

It went up.

I felt my eyes widen.

"NO, NO, NO—"

Buddy's head snapped right in a dry pink mist.

A horrible sob ripped from me as his body slumped forward, blood leaking into the grooves of the plastic. White noise filled my ears. The enforcers immediately began wrapping the body.

"Breathe," Don said. I'd been hyperventilating. "It'll all be over in a second. Would you prefer to stand?"

"*No*—wait—I can—I can—"

"You can what?"

"How much was lost?"

He shrugged. "Let's call it one-sixty."

And clarity returned.

"I can make that."

An enforcer laughed, the sound cut off by Don's immediate subsequent glare.

"No, really, I can," I insisted. "I'm good at what I do. I know people. *Wealthy* people. And one-sixty? Yeah—that's manageable."

Don crouched, intrigued. "Do you *really* believe that, Marcus?"

"I believe I'm your only chance."

Don held my gaze for about five seconds, and in those five seconds I saw a man deliberating—weighing risk against upside, calculating the cost of being wrong in both directions, and listening to the ping in his gut that said I might just be serious and, more frighteningly, correct. Then he blew air through his nose, eyes dipping, and patted me on the shoulder the way a coach pats a kid he's already cut from the roster, and stood back up.

"You ready?"

All composure evaporated.

I started scrambling for my phone on the tarp. "Okay—shit—let me—my father—"

"He knows. Close your eyes."

The world went silent. Not quiet. *Silent.* The kind of silence that swallows everything: traffic, wind, your own heartbeat. My bladder released. I didn't realize it until the warmth spread down my thigh and the smell hit me, and even then it felt like it was happening to someone across the room. My teeth were chattering so hard I thought they'd crack. I tried to pray but couldn't remember a single word of anything—not a verse, not a line, not even the shape of a prayer—just a white hum where language used to be.

My fingers clawed at the tarp beneath me, gripping it like the earth underneath might open up and offer an exit.

It wouldn't.

There was no exit.

There was only me and the man who was about to make me into nothing.

***

I woke up alone in Buddy's apartment.

The plastic, along with Buddy's body, had disappeared. Don was nowhere to be seen.

"Buddy?"

I stood up shakily and looked around the empty room. In the kitchen, I found a note on the counter:

8 A.M. Good luck.

The stove clock read 11 P.M.

Nine hours.

I had nine hours to raise one hundred and sixty-eight thousand dollars or join Buddy in whatever unmarked grave Don had prepared.

I grabbed my keys and ran.

8

THE CLOCK

Time became liquid as I stormed into my apartment, grabbing a JanSport backpack from the coat rack. In my bedroom closet, I yanked clothes off the rack to reveal the safe. I threw all the money, about fifty grand, along with an ounce of coke into the bag.

I changed quickly, trading my club clothes for jeans and a hoodie. I tucked the .45 into my waistband and grabbed a ski mask from my top shelf. The weight of the gun against my skin was reassuring in a way nothing else could be. Nothing else in my life had ever offered that kind of honest promise: not money, not connections, not charm. Just .45-caliber certainty tucked against my spine, the only relationship I had left that didn't require lies or performance art. The gun didn't care about my drunk dad or my moral flexibility. It just waited, ready to solve problems the way problems got solved in the real world—which, as it turned out, was the only world I'd ever actually lived in.

In the guest bedroom, I flipped on the light and shook my father awake.

"Hey. Wake up, Dad."

"Marcus?" He blinked at me, confusion clouding his rheumy eyes.

"Yeah, it's me. We gotta leave right now."

"Huh? What's going on?"

"Nothing. Just trust me, okay?"

He sighed. "Whatever you say."

As I wheeled him out from the apartment, I turned to shut the door only to see Rocco, his big head tilted.

Right. The dog.

***

I drove through the darkened streets of Hollywood in my Range Rover, streetlights blurring into streaks of neon.

My father dozed in the passenger seat, oblivious to the danger we were in. Rocco whined in the back. My mind raced, calculating options, discarding plans almost as quickly as I formed them. This was mathematics at gunpoint: brutal, simple arithmetic where every variable was measured in heartbeats and any miscalculation meant death. Fifty grand plus whatever I could shake out of strip clubs and trust-fund junkies, divided by eight hours, multiplied by the probability that Don Silva was a man of his word about punctuality. The equation kept coming up short, but that was the thing about desperation: it made you believe in impossible math, made you think you could somehow add up to survival when all the numbers pointed toward an unmarked grave.

I needed someplace safe, someplace Don's men wouldn't look immediately. Someplace for my father and Rocco.

Only one person came to mind.

9

GREG

The drive to Hermosa took longer than I had, but peace of mind would go a long way tonight.

I rang the doorbell to her mom's house: beachfront, three stories, Spanish-style. Stephanie opened the door, her expression shifting from surprise to confusion when she saw me standing there.

"What are you doing here?"

I reached behind me and wheeled my father inside. "I know this is a lot to spring on you, but I really need you to take him."

"Wait, what—"

"One second." I disappeared back out into the driveway, returning with Rocco in my arms. "Him, too. I fed him earlier. Please?"

"Are you out of your fucking mind?" Her voice rose an octave.

I dug into my back pocket and produced two pill bottles, holding them up to her eyes. "Put my dad in a dark room with a blanket. A TV would be nice. Give him one of each with a glass of water. You won't hear a word." I glanced around the elegant home.

"Where's your mom?"

"She went out to her friends in Ventura for dinner with my step-dad," Stephanie said, crossing her arms. I heard her nostrils flare as I checked the living room for any excess company. "Were you in a fire? Why do you smell like smoke?"

"Why didn't you go?" I deflected, praying she wouldn't equate the stench to gunpowder.

She scoffed. "What the hell are you doing here?"

"Something bad happened. Really bad. And I have to fix it."

"Marcus..."

"But I'm on a bit of a timetable. So I'm asking you... as a *friend*, to please shelter my father, and maybe pet Rocco a little bit." I gestured to Rocco, who was panting. "He's a little agitated."

"What about Buddy?"

I moved to close the curtains, avoiding her eyes. "He's in Mexico. Seeing family."

"Stephanie?"

We both turned to see a bland, affable-looking yuppie type standing at the foot of the stairs. Greg. Stephanie's new boyfriend. Of course.

"Who's this?" I asked, though I already knew.

"His name's Greg." The defensive note in her voice told me everything I needed to know about their relationship status.

"Greg. Oh, as in... Right." I swallowed the vicious comments that sprang to my mind. "Hey, man. I'm Marcus. The ex."

"What's going on?" Greg's attempt at assertiveness might have been amusing under different circumstances. Now, it was just annoying.

"Don't sweat it, Greg. Just asking a little favor of Stephanie." I tried to keep my tone neutral, non-threatening.

"Woah." Greg turned to Stephanie, ignoring me. "You okay, babe?"

"She's fine," I snapped, patience fraying.

"Forgive me if I don't want to take your word for it."

I lurched toward him, meeting his eyes directly—too aggressive. "Yeah? Why's that?"

"Marcus."

She was right. I was about to blow this whole night over ego. I backed off. "Just give us a minute, okay? You'll have her back in a moment."

Stephanie gave Greg a nod of reassurance. Greg nodded and left. "I'll be in the kitchen, babe."

"Really? Him?" I couldn't help myself.

"He's nice. He listens. Also, who are you to say anything? You barge in here full of demands with your gigantic dog and sick dad, try to fight my boyfriend, and now you want to shit on my life?"

Fair.

"Look, I'm sorry, okay? I'm just on edge. Now, if anybody knocks that isn't your parents, don't open it."

"I don't like this."

"You think I do?"

"This is *your* mess."

Again, fair. I adjusted my tone.

"You're right. And the last thing I'd want to do is make it yours or Greg's. I'm just asking for a little help. Alright? I promise I'll make it up to you."

"Don't make any more promises you can't keep." She looked at me with a mixture of pity and resignation. That *look*: I'd seen it before, in Dr. Mann's office, in my father's eyes before the drinking finally broke him, in my own reflection during those 3 A.M. moments when the cocaine wore off and I had to face what I'd become. It was the look you give someone who's already dead but hasn't stopped moving yet. The look reserved for lost causes and walking disasters, for the clinically insane, for people who've crossed so many lines they can't find their way back to human. Stephanie was looking at me like I was a ghost, and maybe I was.

As I headed for the door, she added: "You're a real dick, you know that?"

"Well aware," I replied. The admission was strangely liberating.

I knew where to go. The Garden of Eden Gentlemen's Club—where Buddy had lost our product.

If there was anything left to salvage, it began there.

10

OVERTIME

I parked across the street from the club, engine off. The club pulsed dimly behind tinted glass.

I saw him immediately. Dark skin, black blazer, cigarette glowing as he paced the curb with a phone to his ear.

Freddy Green, CPA. *Certified Professional Asshole.*

And owner of this dump.

Now I remembered.

I'd seen him float through a dozen parties over the years—never invited, always arriving like the human equivalent of a plumbing leak. Always sniffed out the bathroom first, locked the door, did rails alone like he was too good to share, then thumbed through his phone looking for girls with braces in their profile pictures. If he wasn't in there, you can bet he was *outside*, arguing with whatever poor kid from Allied was working the door that night—usually some twenty-year-old Black kid named Jamal with one AirPod in—about how they "had no fuckin' idea who he knew."

Yeah, you tell 'em, Freddy.

The thing about LA? You think you've met the worst of it, and then Freddy strolls into your line of view. He wasn't dangerous in the way I was used to—guns, debt, bodies in the trunk—but there was a darkness to him. A kind that doesn't get you killed quick. It works slower. Seeps in through your skin. Leaves you just like him.

"The house is already in escrow," he was saying as I approached the bouncer, hoodie pulled low over my head. "I mean, I don't know what to tell this guy..."

"How much?" I asked, nodding toward the entrance.

"We're at capacity." The mountain of a man didn't even bother to look at me directly.

"What?"

"You deaf, slow, or in between? I said we're at capacity. Beat it, *Zack & Cody*."

Freddy hung up and walked over. "Problem, Maurice?"

"I'm trying to tell dude over here we're full." He jerked a thumb in my direction.

"That's just legal bullshit. He's fine." Freddy winked at me. "Have fun, kid."

"Twenty bucks," the bouncer grumbled, stepping aside.

Inside, the club pulsed with cheap music and expensive fantasies. I took the first seat available in front of the stage and settled in to wait, watching Freddy as he passed by, complimenting some of the dancers before disappearing into a hallway past the bar. Through the dim lighting, I could see him arguing with a young redheaded stripper.

"Hey." A voice pulled my attention back to the stage.

A stripper with black hair and an hourglass figure was eyeing me with professional interest.

I leaned forward, using the interaction to keep my face hidden. "What's your name?"

"Sapphire." Her smile was practiced, automatic.

"That's not your name."

She chuckled, charmed. "Jessica."

"Well," I said, placing my arms on the stage railing, "something very bad happened to me tonight, Jessica."

"Poor baby." She unclasped her bra and started playing with her breasts. "I'll give you a discount. Two-for-one. Back room."

"You would do that for me?" I said, unabashedly coy.

"Just for the cute ones."

I glanced back toward Freddy, who was now yelling at the redhead. He threw a handful of bills at her face and slapped her, then stormed out of sight down a hallway.

Green light.

"Rain check, sweetheart," I said, already moving away from the stage. The whole place reeked of desperation masquerading as desire—middle-aged men pretending twenty-dollar bills bought them more than theatrical intimacy, girls pretending the whole gig was temporary. It was Los Angeles in microcosm. Everyone selling, everyone buying, *everyone lying*.

I assumed the direction Freddy had gone, finding myself outside an office door marked MANAGEMENT. I pulled the ski mask down over my face, took a deep breath, and entered without knocking.

Freddy was pouring a drink, classic rock playing from his desktop speakers. He looked at me, absurdly unfazed by the masked intruder.

"No refunds, bud. What's with the mask? Chicks dig that shit?" He giggled at his own remark.

I slowly raised my .45, aiming the trembling barrel at his chest. The humor drained from his face.

"Oh."

I locked the door behind me with my free hand.

"Let me guess. You're the *other* guy Freddy's demeanor shifted to calculated casualness. "Shit, I've bought from you. That Buddy kid, he'd get fucked up, throw hundreds, buy the bar. Mention you. Not the brightest bulb, but I like him. He knows how to have fun. I had a feeling out there at the door. You just looked like such a fucking schlub that I had to second guess. I mean, what's the matter? You get fired? Just kidding. Seriously, though, what was your name again? Marcus... *Graves*, right?"

Jesus, that was quick.

"Where's the coke?" I kept my voice steady, the gun less so.

Freddy laughed, the sound harsh and mocking. "What, you thought I'd just have it neatly wrapped and awaiting your arrival? What are you? The Coke Duke of LA, coming to collect?"

He scoffed, circled around his desk. "It's gone, man. Want a drink?"

"What?" The word came out strangled.

"Jesus, you really are slow. It's *gone*. G-O-N-E. The shit you're talking about? Presto change-o. It doesn't exist anymore."

"Then give me everything in the safe." I nodded toward the large metal box in the corner of the office.

His eyes narrowed, assessing me. "You got some fucking balls, kid."

"Open it."

"Now, why the fuck would I do that? That thing even loaded?"

I didn't answer, letting the question hang in the air between us.

"Fine." Freddy raised his hands mockingly and took a step toward the safe. "I'll open it, tough guy."

I glanced quickly at the door.

Mistake.

In that split second of distraction, Freddy lunged at me with surprising speed, a fully-ejected switchblade appearing in his hand. I felt the burn as the blade sank into my arm.

We wrestled against the wall clumsily, knocking over file cabinets and bulletin boards until I finally mustered the strength to whack him in the face with the butt of the .45. Freddy crumpled, dazed, leaning against his desk for support. Rage and pain fueled me as I continued to repeatedly beat him with the gun handle, each impact making a sickening sound against his skull.

"THAT FEEL FUCKING LOADED ENOUGH FOR YOU?!" I shouted, adrenaline making my voice shake.

Realizing I couldn't obtain the code from a dead man, I separated from him and picked up the knife that had fallen to the ground. I pocketed it, then turned up Freddy's stereo—"Good Times, Bad Times" by Led Zeppelin.

I aimed the gun at him again as he spat blood and teeth onto the carpet. The barrel was steady now.

"Shit, man..." Freddy held his jaw, stunned by the violence. His gaze stopped at my feet. I looked down.

A pool of blood forming.

Freddy laughed, a wet, gurgling sound through his broken teeth. "That don't look too good."

"Shut the fuck up," I snarled, kicking him in the stomach.

While he was winded, I found a roll of duct tape in one of the drawers and used my teeth to tear off a piece, wrapping it around my bicep as a makeshift tourniquet. Kicked Freddy again just as he had caught his breath, just for the pain.

"Open the fucking safe."

"Alright, alright," he wheezed, crawling toward the safe on hands and knees after unfolding from a pretzel.

As Freddy dialed the combination, a heavy knock sounded at the door. My heart nearly stopped.

"Everything okay in there, big man?"

Maurice.

I pressed the barrel harder against Freddy's temple. "Tell him you're talking to your mother," I whispered urgently.

"My mother's dead, you prick," Freddy hissed back.

"Tell him you're jerking off, then. I don't give a fuck. I *will* fucking kill you, do you understand?"

Freddy raised his voice, straining for normalcy. "Hey, uh, it's all good, Mo. Just moving some shelves."

Silence.

"...Alright, man."

Heavy footsteps retreated down the hallway.

"Hurry the fuck up," I urged, relief making me momentarily

dizzy.

"I'm doing it. *Jesus*."

While Freddy worked the combination, I noticed his bloody handprint on a dancer's promotional photo. "You shouldn't hit the girls."

"What?" He looked up, genuinely bewildered.

"I said you shouldn't hit the girls."

He stared at me, then shook his head and returned to the safe. "You're a weird guy, man."

CLACK! The safe door swung open, revealing stacks of cash inside.

"Take it all out."

Freddy strained to reach into the safe, pulling out bundles of bills one by one. "Ten grand, ten grand, ten grand... fifty grand. *There*. Happy, you fucking prick?"

"Where's the rest of it?"

"Fuck you!" he squealed. "That's fifty grand! It's all I have, you understand?"

His indignation was adorable.

I hit him in the face with the pistol again, splitting his eyebrow open. "Where's the rest of the money?"

"*Ow!* Fuck! I just told you! That's it!" Blood streamed down his face, pooling with the rest on the carpet.

"There were seven kilos, you piece of shit!"

"And we sold *four*. The rest of the money... it's elsewhere." Freddy's eyes darted to the side—maybe a tell, maybe brain damage. "I don't know what to tell you. Maybe you should try consulting with your dumbfuck partner. You're the one with the connects, right? How about *you* figure the rest out, Scarface?"

"How'd you lift it?"

"Well, that remedial case wouldn't stop talking about it. We fed him drinks, had the girls occupy him in the back, and Maurice went out with a crowbar. It was in the *trunk*, for Christ's sake—"

"You realize who you stole from, you fucking moron? Who has

it?"

Freddy just started laughing, a broken, manic sound. I whacked him again, harder this time. The laughter turned into a pained sob.

"Goddammit, man! You're gonna fuckin' kill me!"

"Who?"

"This dumb rich kid. Some fuckin' Jew, goes by White Lightning' or some shit. Trevor something. Trust-fund baby. The raging drug-addict type."

I froze. "You said White Lightning?"

"Yeah. That fucking psycho came in and offered to buy it all. What was I gonna say?" He studied my silence. "You know the moron, don't you?"

Unfortunately, I did. Trevor Horowitz: regular customer, tech money family, lived in the Hills, and the kind of guy whose obituary you'd read twice just to make sure.

Freddy Green had just handed me my lifeline.

"Can I keep my money now?" Freddy asked, hopeful.

"Fuck you." I grabbed a Walgreens bag from behind his desk and threw it on the floor. "Fill it up."

***

After Freddy had packed the cash, I zip-tied his hands behind a chair.

"Keys," I demanded.

"Left pocket."

I dug into his pocket and retrieved his car keys. Leaning close to his ear, I hissed: "And my name's not fucking Marcus."

"Best of luck, douchebag," he replied, defiant to the end.

I locked the office door behind me and made my way through the backstage area, lifting my mask as I passed confused dancers. Outside, I threw the money and mask into the backseat of the Range Rover, wincing as adrenaline dumped and pain rocketed in my arm. The makeshift duct tape bandage was already soaked through with blood.

As I inserted my key into the ignition, something danced in my peripheral vision. I turned my head to discover a large Black man was racing toward me. For a split-second, I couldn't believe it, looking away and then looking back again.

Maurice, the enormous bouncer, charging my car with a pump-action shotgun that looked like a water pistol in his hands.

I floored it just as he fired.

BOOM! BOOM! Two shells shattered my rear window as I sped into an intersection.

I didn't see the taxi until it was too late.

The impact was deafening, metal crumpling against metal as the cab T-boned my car. Physics doesn't negotiate. Doesn't care about your deadline or your daddy in a wheelchair or the dog you left in someone else's care. Physics just *is*—momentum and mass and the absolute certainty that when two objects occupy the same space, something's got to fucking give. In this case, it was my consciousness, my timeline, and probably my last real chance at staying breathing past sunrise. The universe had just served me an eviction notice, and I was about to find out if I had any appeals left.

My head met steering wheel, and everything went black.

11

GIVE ME A CIGARETTE

I came to consciousness against something soft.

The world swam back into focus slowly: first shapes, then colors, then the concerned face of Ricky Atwater hovering above me. He had a fresh black eye, one I hoped hadn't come from me.

"Dude, thank God," he said, pressing a cold pack against my forehead. "I was starting to wonder if you were dead."

I was on his couch, the fabric beneath me sticky with blood—mine, presumably. "Where am I?"

"My place. You remember calling me?"

I shook my head, which proved to be a mistake as pain lanced through my skull. "Last thing I remember is the crash."

"Yeah, well, you're lucky you could even dial a phone. Some Mexican dudes were heading toward your car when I pulled up. You were barely conscious, mumbling about needing to get to the Hollywood Hills."

I tried to sit up, failed, then tried again with Ricky's help. "What time is it?"

"Almost 2 A.M."

Four hours. I had four hours to find Trevor, get the coke or the cash, and make it to Don's meet-up. The odds were grim, but they were better than they had been an hour ago.

"I need your help," I said.

Ricky looked at my bloodied arm, my bruised face. "No shit, Einstein. You need a hospital is what you need."

"No hospitals." I gripped his wrist with surprising strength. "I need to get to Trevor Horowitz's place in the Hills."

"White Lightning? That dude is bad news, man. Last time I went to one of his parties, someone OD'd in the pool house. Motherfucker just had it drained and refilled while the body was still warm."

"He has something I need. Something worth more than money."

Ricky's eyes narrowed with understanding. "*That's* what this is about? You trying to jack Trevor?"

"Complicated."

Ricky whistled low. "Boy, you must be out yo' mind."

I gestured to my arm. "Can you help me with this?"

"Let me see." He disappeared into his bathroom for a moment and returned with a first aid kit. "Shit got real, huh?"

"You have no idea."

As Ricky cleaned and stitched my arm, his hands steadier than I would have expected, he filled me in on his own recent troubles.

"We got robbed last week. That's how this happened." He pointed to his black eye. "Some kids from the projects. Took my stash, my roommate's cash. Now I'm stuck paying double rent because the fucking pussy went back to Wisconsin."

I watched him work as I listened. "How'd it happen?"

Ricky paused, needle suspended in the air. "You really wanna hear this dumbass shit right now?"

"Better than thinking about what's coming next."

He resumed stitching, his voice taking on the flat quality people use when recounting trauma—or nonsense. "Alright, so last Saturday night, my girl Tatianna had some people over. Nothing crazy, just some friends getting fucked up, you know? I got off work at nine. Stopped by an ARCO for some cigarettes 'cause she said we needed some."

He tied off a stitch, testing the tension. "I come in, right? People go *nuts*. The second I hold 'em up, this little black kid—maybe nineteen, never seen him once in my life—standing in the back corner goes, 'Give me a cigarette.' All loud and shit. Room goes silent. And I'm thinking, I don't really like his tone, but then he comes over and starts telling me about how he just got out of jail and all this shit, so I give him the benefit of the doubt and give him one, you know? I'd want a cigarette if I just got out, too.

"And then I'm like, 'Fuck it,' and I start handing everybody one. The crowd's loving it. So, you know, we're partying: taking shots, smoking cigarettes, taking rips, doing a little coke. Around eleven, it starts to die down a bit. People want to hit the bars, get some greasy food, keep the night going. They start to clear out."

Ricky dabbed some alcohol on my arm. "And me, well, I'm *drunk* at this point. I wanna lie down. So Donnie goes into the next room, and I go get in bed with Tatianna. We fuck for a little, take some rips, then I take my end, and I close my eyes."

He paused, touching his black eye unconsciously. "An hour later, I hear this banging. Someone's knocking, and I remember being really fucking thirsty, so I started pounding this Pedialyte shit that Donnie gave me, and I almost choke because the shit goes down like fucking cough syrup. I walk over to the door. I open it. Nobody's on the steps, but it's quiet, *real* quiet. My eyes adjust, and I see some dude, wearing a hoodie and standing directly across from my apartment, just staring. And, you know, I can barely make out his face, so I'm like, 'What the fuck? Can I help you?' He doesn't say anything. He's just standing there, all creepy and shit. Then I hear someone's shoes scraping against the sidewalk."

Ricky's voice dropped lower, more intense. "I take two steps out the door, look down to the left, and there he is: the same fucking kid that pressed me for a cigarette. And he's all fucked up, mumbling, slipping against the damn railing. I try to get his attention. He looks at me, and he just goes...

"'Give me a cigarette.'"

"Jesus."

"At this point, I just figure the kid's fucking demented or something, and I go to close the door. You know, laughing it off, literally. The second I move, they start running on some *Dawn of the Dead*, *30 Days of Night* type shit. I slam the door, double-latch it, all that shit. Within three seconds, they're going fucking crazy on it. Yelling, banging, cussing, waking up all of Santa Monica. I go into my room to get my gun, but I can't find the fucking thing. Before I know it, minutes have passed, my girl's tripping, and these motherfuckers are still at my door. Then I hear Donnie's door open."

Ricky shook his head. "Mind you, this kid Donnie's from Wisconsin where, like, fucking nothing bad happens, so he's practically *skipping* to the door to let these motherfuckers in. I slam my toe on a coffee table leg as I'm running over to Donnie, so hard that the leg snaps in two, leaving me completely fucking incapacitated. And I'm just screaming, 'DON'T OPEN THE FUCKING DOOR!' But I'm too late. He lets 'em in.

"Long story short, they bust in, push bitch-ass Donnie over, and punch me in the goddamn face—and I mean *punched*. Took everything. The cigarettes, my stash under the TV, Donnie's rent money, even some of my food—two brand new boxes of Lucky Charms—just to be dicks about it." He finished the last stitch and stepped back to admire his work. "Donnie packed up the next morning. Said he couldn't handle the stress. Almost swung on bruh."

Under different circumstances, it might've been the funniest thing I'd ever heard. Instead, I gave him a faint, lopsided smile and a nod, conserving my oxygen.

"Can you drive?" I asked once the silence had stretched long enough.

"Yeah, but your car is toast. We'll have to take mine."

***

We headed out, the iron security gate clanging shut behind us. We moved down the exterior walkway, the dry L.A. air pressing in as we descended the concrete stairs to the back lot.

I froze halfway down, my hand white-knuckling the rusted rail. For a heart-stopping second, I thought a SWAT team had the lot boxed in. Sitting deep in the shadows of the corner was a reinforced, blacked-out monster of a truck, sporting a police-style grille guard that looked built for an urban war zone or an apocalypse.

Then Ricky clicked the fob, and the blue LEDs flashed.

"Pretty sick, right?" he asked, his voice echoing off the stucco walls with a note of unmistakable pride.

I looked at the heavy steel-plated front end, then back at him. "Is that even legal?"

Ricky just laughed, hauling the heavy door open. "Man, I know you ain't just ask me that. Get in the truck."

***

The drive to Trevor's place passed in a haze of pain and planning. I knew I would need to be at my sharpest to handle what was coming, but my body had other ideas. Every pothole sent waves of agony through my battered frame.

"So what's the plan?" Ricky asked as we approached the exclusive neighborhood where Trevor lived.

"We talk to him. Make him understand the situation. Best case, he gives us what we need, and everyone walks away happy."

"And worst case?"

I could feel the .45 pressing against my spine, the weight of it suddenly more pronounced, like it was responding to Ricky's question with metallic eagerness. The gun seemed to pulse with its own heartbeat, reminding me it was there, ready, waiting for the moment when talking stopped working.

"Let's hope it doesn't come to that."

We drove the rest of the way in silence.

12

COKE, PILL, WEED? EMERGEN-C?

Trevor's house was exactly what you'd expect from someone with too much money and not enough sense: a modernist nightmare perched on the edge of a cliff, all glass and angles and fuck-you excess. Music thumped from inside despite the late hour, the bass vibrating through the ground beneath our feet. It looked like what happened when you gave unlimited money to someone with the emotional development of a thirteen-year-old, the kind of place that existed solely to impress people who confused expensive with interesting, conspicuous with meaningful. Trevor's entire existence was performance art, a trust fund kid playing dress-up as a dangerous person while real danger circled him like sharks. He just didn't know he was bleeding yet.

"Let me do the talking," I told Ricky as we approached the front door.

Trevor Horowitz opened the door himself—a sickly-looking pale kid the height of a Duke point guard with short blonde hair, donning a silk Versace robe over Spider-Man boxers, whose malnutrition betrayed his length grotesquely. He was sweating profusely, his pupils dilated to the size of dimes. I could smell the vodka and all the shit I had cut his coke with.

"Marky-Mark! Twice in one night? How'd I get so lucky?" His grin was manically wide, yellowed teeth grinding slightly as he spoke.

"Hey, Trevor…" I tried to sound casual despite my battered appearance.

"Come in, fellas."

"It's not too late?" I asked, noting the hour with faux politeness as if this maniac ever slept.

"Never too late for you, brother bear."

Trevor led us into a living room where two young women, one black, one white, sat on a couch, looking bored and stoned. Champagne bottles and lines of cocaine dotted the glass coffee table.

"Sugar, Honey! Why don't you make a little room for my guests?" Trevor called to them.

"Their names are Sugar and Honey?" Ricky asked, tragically green.

"No, dickhead. They're whores." Trevor rolled his eyes. "Anyway, you guys want a drink or something? Coke, pill, weed? Emergen-C?"

I jumped in. "We're fine. Trevor, we gotta talk—"

"Yeah, yeah, cool, man. Let's just do some coke first. Gotta get my mind right." He sat on the couch and leaned over the coffee table, snorting a line with practiced efficiency. "Fuck, that's some primo shit. So what are you up to tonight, Marcus? Slinging rock and cock as per usual?"

"You know how it is," I said flatly, trying to play along while surveying the room for signs of what I was looking for.

"So, what's going on? You guys have something for me?" Trevor's eyes darted between us expectantly, reptilian.

"Not right now."

"Just passing through? No problem." He sniffed hard, rubbing his nose. "Any friend of Marcus' is a friend of mine. You guys want a sippy sip?"

Before we could answer, Trevor shot up and circled to his bar, mixing drinks we hadn't asked for. "You should've dropped in earlier, Marcus. I mean, you want to talk about fucking mayhem..." He walked back with a tray of cocktails. "This one skank was so coked up. She thought her boyfriend was cheating on her. Talking to some other bimbo by the pool, right? So, what does she do? Grabs a *knife* from my kitchen and charges him like a fucking rhino or something. The guy jukes—played for USC, mind you—and she goes flying face-first into my patio. She rolls over, and guess what?"

"What?" I asked, playing along.

"Knife's in her fucking side! Bingo!"

"Jesus!"

"For-real?" Ricky looked genuinely shocked.

"So much blood. Slasher movie status. And she knocked all her fucking teeth out. Bitch went from an LA seven to a Bakersfield six. Pain in the ass getting it out of the concrete. I had Sugar and some other chick throw her in an Uber to Cedars. You know, drop her at the curb so I didn't have to deal with the pigs. Anyway, what did you wanna talk about?"

"I'd prefer somewhere more private," I suggested.

"Copy that." He grinned at the women. "Ladies, keep my friend's friend company. Gotta talk some business."

Trevor grabbed his drink and led me to his bedroom, leaving Ricky with the two girls.

The master bedroom was a disaster zone of rumpled sheets, discarded clothes, and—you guessed it—more coke. Trevor sat on his unmade bed, sipping his cocktail.

"What's the deal, player?"

"You know Freddy Green, Trevor? The strip club owner?" I kept my voice casual, though my heart was racing.

"Sure. Why?"

"There's no easy way to say this, but Freddy fucked up." I spoke slowly, speaking slowly as if to a child while navigating the communicative triplines of the perpetually privileged to ensure my words actually penetrated his chemical haze. "He stole some shit from the wrong people, and now they're pissed. Because it didn't belong to him. It belonged to them; and, by proxy, me. Now, I know Freddy sold you some blow. Four kilos, specifically, and I don't know what you're—"

"Hey, where's that other guy? The little one. Got, like, a dog's name or some shit? Buster?" Trevor's attention had already wandered.

"Trevor. I need you to focus." I fought to keep my voice—and fists—level. "It's in the best interests of a certain party to retain what you were given, and quickly. If they have to come themselves, they won't be nice. Not like me."

Trevor stared at me blankly. I'd used too many words. "So, like... what are you saying, man? It doesn't belong to me?"

"Yes. That's exactly what I'm saying."

"But I bought it." His confusion seemed genuine, like a toddler struggling with the concept of sharing.

"Listen, I can make this worth your while—"

"Don't take this the wrong way, but maybe you should take better care of your product. I mean, shit happens, right?"

I started walking toward him, patience evaporating, when something in the corner of my eye stopped me cold. We both turned our heads—slowly—toward the bathroom door, where a terrible sight greeted us.

A bloodied young woman, lying naked and unconscious in the bathtub.

My pulse slowed.

"Trevor... What the *fuck* is that?!" My voice rose to a shout.

"It's nothing." He shrugged, as if we were discussing a stain on the carpet.

"That's not nothing! Who is that?!"

"I don't know."

"WHAT DO YOU MEAN YOU DON'T KNOW?!"

"It was earlier, man. We were doing coke and just hanging out. I was playing her my mixtape—*The Chronicles of T-Dogg*, eight tracks, no features, on SoundCloud—and, out of nowhere, she started tweaking. Bleeding from her nose and shit, crawling around on my floor—"

"Is she dead?" The question came out in a horrified whisper.

"I don't know, actually." Trevor looked toward the bathroom with mild curiosity.

"You didn't check?!"

"I told you, Marcus. I had a lot of people here. *Important* people." His tone suggested this explained everything. Then his eyes shifted—just slightly—and you could see it: the flicker of a thought he didn't like having.

His gaze lingered at my feet now, despondent. I felt the temperature in the room plummet to the sub-zero chill of irreversibility.

"Please don't tell anybody about this."

"What the hell is wrong with you, man?!"

"I fucked up, didn't I?" For a moment, genuine fear crossed Trevor's face.

"Yeah. A little."

The understatement of the fucking century. Trevor had graduated from recreational sociopathy to accidental homicide, and his biggest concern was whether his daddy would be disappointed. It was like watching someone worry about a parking ticket while their house burned down around them. But that was the thing about guys like Trevor—they lived in a consequence-free bubble for so long that when reality finally punctured it, they had no idea how to process actual stakes. Death was just another mess for someone else to clean up, another problem money could solve, until suddenly it wasn't.

Trevor reached into his robe pocket and pulled out a vial, dumping about six lines' worth of cocaine onto his nightstand. Before I could register what was unfolding, he grabbed a pre-rolled dollar bill from his breast pocket like it was a pocket pistol.

I lurched. "Wait, wait, wait—"

And snorted it all in one go.

"Oh my fucking God." I watched in quiet horror as his eyes rolled back briefly, then refocused.

"I'm sorry, Marcus," he mumbled, swaying slightly.

"Look, just give me the shit and I'll forget this ever happened."

"I'm a terrible person, aren't I?" Trevor's voice had gone dreamy, distant.

"Trevor, I need the coke. Otherwise, I'm gonna have no choice but to send these people your way; the people that killed my friend, the people that wanna kill me—"

Not listening, Trevor reached into the drawer of his nightstand and revealed his closing argument—a .44 Magnum. I backed up immediately, hands raised.

"Dude, what the fuck are you doing?"

"I let you down, didn't I?" Tears welled in his bloodshot eyes.

"Trevor, give me the gun."

Trevor ran into the bathroom and slammed the door.

"Trevor, come out of there," I called through the door, panic rising.

"You're just gonna try and stop me," he said, muffled through the wood.

"Look, I'll go find you a Valium or something. Just sit on the bed and give me the gun."

"I'm a murderer, Marcus. Can't you see? Oh my God, my dad's gonna kill me—"

"It was an accident. We'll figure it out together." I tried to keep my voice soothing.

"Marcus?" His voice had changed, suddenly becoming child-like.

"What?"

"I feel weird. My heart, it's like... one beat..."

I realized what was happening. "Trevor, open the door!" I pounded on the wood.

BANG.

The gunshot was deafening in the enclosed space. Silence fell, heavy and final.

"Fuck!"

Trevor's phone began to ring on the nightstand: "Ass, titties, ass and titties! Ass, titties, ass and titties!"

Even in death, Trevor managed to be embarrassing. The ringtone was like a final fuck-you from the universe, a reminder that this wasn't some noble tragedy, just another rich kid's drug-fueled suicide scored to strip club anthems.

I glanced at the screen: *F-Money*.

Freddy.

Freed.

I picked up the phone and answered. A beat of silence.

"Yo, Lightning." Freddy's voice came through, slightly slurred.

I remained silent, calculating my next move.

"You there, man?" Freddy prompted.

"Yeah," I replied softly, disguising my voice.

From Freddy's end came the metallic sound of a .45 being loaded. "Hey, listen, I gotta drop in real quick. Some shit went down and, uh... we just gotta talk, alright?"

My blood ran cold.

"That cool? Got anybody over?"

I hung up without answering. The silence that followed felt loaded with inevitability. Freddy was coming with Maurice and God knows who else, armed and pissed off about the brain damage I'd given him. We had minutes, maybe less, before this turned into a shooting gallery with us as the targets. Every second spent searching was a second closer to becoming corpses ourselves.

I started tearing the room apart.

"RICKY!" I bellowed.

Ricky appeared in the doorway, eyes wide. "What the fuck happened?"

"Trevor's dead. We need to find the coke or cash, now. Check the mattress."

Ricky pulled out a knife and sliced the mattress open. White feathers exploded into the air as we frantically searched the gutted bedding. We looked like we were trapped inside a snow globe designed by a paranoid schizophrenic—white feathers drifting through the air while we tore apart a dead man's bedroom looking for enough drugs to keep us alive. The absurdity wasn't lost on me, even in the moment. This was my life now: grave robbing with a timer, racing against armed degenerates while drowning in goose down.

Nothing.

I grabbed Ricky by the shoulders: "TEAR THIS HOUSE APART!"

"And the girls?"

I could've throttled him.

"FUCK THE GIRLS! GET THEM OUT!"

Ricky nodded and sprinted out of the room. I continued searching Trevor's bedroom closet when—

BAM! BAM!

Two bullets pierced the bathroom door.

I dove behind the bed for cover.

BOOM! The bathroom door burst open, and the young woman from the tub staggered out, swinging Trevor's revolver wildly. Blood covered her naked body. She screamed incoherently and fired another round into the ceiling.

"ARE YOU FUCKING KIDDING ME?!" I shouted, ducking lower. Because of course she wasn't dead. Of course the *one* person who should have been a corpse was now wielding Trevor's cannon and trying to redecorate the bedroom with my brain matter.

She tripped over the bed frame and tumbled directly onto me. We wrestled for the gun, which proved horrifyingly difficult. Her grip was like steel cables, powered by whatever speedball cocktail was keeping her upright despite massive blood loss. Wrestling with her was like fighting a zombie—all mechanical strength and no self-preservation, just pure chemical momentum driving a body that should have been dead hours ago.

I managed to slap her hard and throw her off, then sprinted for the door.

This was what happened when chaos met chemistry—a naked, blood-covered woman firing a .44 Magnum at random while high on whatever cocktail of stimulants was coursing through her system. It was like something out of a David Lynch fever dream, except Lynch would have had the good sense to make it metaphorical. This was just my Los Angeles on a Tuesday night, where the line between surreal and deadly disappeared entirely, where someone's overdose became someone else's attempted murder charge. The town specialized in these kinds of transitions, turning victims into chemically-enhanced perpetrators.

In the living room, Ricky was tearing apart the couch, finding nothing. The young woman stumbled after me, firing a fourth round blindly.

"Please handle her!" I yelled, diving into the kitchen as plaster rained.

From the corner of my eye, I saw Ricky grab an empty champagne and beam it like a ghetto Aaron Rodgers at the feral woman. BONK! Her head snapped back, legs kicking into the air like a cartoon and the back of her skull smacking the marble with the sound of a coconut dropped from ten stories.

The sound was final in a way Trevor's gunshot hadn't been—wet, decisive, the kind of noise that let you know someone's evening was officially over. Ricky stood over her for a moment, champagne bottle still in hand, looking like he couldn't quite believe what he'd just done. Welcome to the club, I thought. Population: everyone who'd ever met me.

I frantically searched the kitchen drawers, finding nothing but takeout menus and utensils. I froze dead in my tracks, a realization hitting me.

"He doesn't cook."

I rushed to the oven and tore out the upper and lower grates. There, hidden inside, were five bricks of cocaine and stacks of cash.

"Gotta be at least one-fifty. Holy shit..." Relief washed over me. "We're golden, baby!"

For exactly ten seconds, I believed in happy endings. The money was there, the product was intact, and maybe—just maybe—I could walk away from this nightmare with enough cash to satisfy Don Silva and keep breathing past sunrise. It was a beautiful thirty seconds, full of possibility and hope and all the other shit that gets you killed in America.

Ricky looked up from the woman he'd wandered over to inspect, a faint smile forming on his lips. Then his expression changed to one of terror as his eyes shot to the door, sensing something I couldn't. I heard it then: the scrape of footsteps on concrete, the low murmur of voices coordinating an assault. Ricky's street instincts had kicked in before mine, his body already tensing for violence while I was still processing the sounds of our execution approaching. Too late to run, too late to hide, too late to do anything but watch Maurice's shotgun swing toward us like the hand of fate.

BANG!

The front door flew open. Maurice stood in the doorway, shotgun aimed directly at Ricky. Without hesitation, he fired twice at point-blank range.

Time became elastic, stretching that moment into forever. I could see the muzzle flash, hear the shotgun's roar, watch Ricky's body jerk backwards like he'd been hit by an invisible truck.

I shoved everything into a backpack and scrambled for an exit. Slipping on Trevor's blood, I crashed through a window instead, landing face-first onto the patio.

"Bitch ass nigga!" Maurice's voice boomed after me from inside. BOOM! BOOM!

Windows shattered around me as I dashed past the LED-lit pool to the edge of the patio. The pool lights cast everything in an artificial blue glow, like we were performing this chase scene underwater. Even Trevor's backyard was a stage set, designed for maximum visual impact with minimum substance. I was running for my life through a fucking Instagram post.

Freddy and Maurice were closing in fast. I turned to face them, ready to make my stand, when I tripped over a lounge chair and fell backwards into the steep hillside.

I tumbled down the slope, the backpack coming undone, loose cash flying into the night air. Money fluttered around me like confetti at the world's worst party; hundreds and fifties spinning through the darkness, my salvation scattered to the winds by gravity and poor coordination.

After what felt like an eternity of impact and pain, I came to a halt in a brush, face-down and still.

13

BEAUTIFUL FAMILY

I slowly lifted my head, vision swimming. Through the haze, I made out a figure: a man sitting poolside at a neighboring property, smoking a cigarette and watching me with a detached curiosity.

"Help me," I tried to say, but only a groan emerged.

The man took another drag, considering me like an interesting insect. Then he stood and approached, his movements unhurried. He was tall. Skinny. Black hair cut short and simple at Supercuts.

"You're in bad shape," he observed, crouching beside me. "Thomas Berkshire. I'm a doctor."

"Marcus," I managed weakly, tasting blood. The metallic tang coated my tongue like a communion wafer made of failure. Everything hurt in that specific way that let you know your body was seriously reconsidering its commitment to keeping you alive. But there was something almost peaceful about lying there in the dirt, looking up at this stranger who'd found me broken at the bottom of his world. For the first time in months, someone was offering help without calculating what they could get in return.

He flicked the cigarette. "Let's get you inside."

***

The study walls were decorated with various certificates, trophies, and pictures related to the field of medicine. With practiced hands, he examined my injuries.

"So you just fell?" he asked, his tone suggesting he knew I was full of shit.

"Basically." I winced as he probed a particularly tender spot.

"You live up there?" He nodded toward Trevor's house, barely visible above the slope.

"No."

"Your heart's pounding."

"High blood pressure. Got my old man to thank for it, I guess." I tried for humor, failed miserably.

"A one-seventy BPM isn't exactly something to write off." Thomas set his stethoscope down and began feeling around my chest area. "I'm going to prod a little bit. Just tell me what hurts

"There," I gasped as his fingers found a broken rib.

"From what I can tell, you have three broken ribs, a severe pectoral strain, and a surefire concussion. Haven't even checked your pelvic area yet."

"I can walk."

"Give it a few." His voice was kind but firm. "You're a young guy. You want to be using a cane for the rest of your natural life?"

"I don't think so." I managed a weak smile.

"Doesn't go over particularly well with the ladies, I'll tell you that much." Thomas moved back to his desk.

A little boy appeared at the door, staring at me with unblinking fascination.

"Norman, it's bedtime," Thomas admonished gently.

The boy looked at his father, then back at me. I smiled and shot him a wink.

"Norman. You know your mother would kill me if she knew I let you stay up late again."

"Okay, Daddy."

"Good boy. I'll see you in the morning."

Thomas kissed his son's forehead and sent him off to bed. I noticed a stack of Christmas cards on his desk and picked one up. It featured Thomas, Norman, an elegant woman, and a yellow Labrador, all posed by their backyard pool.

"May I?" I asked, holding up the card.

Thomas nodded. I studied the image, feeling a strange hollowness inside.

"You have a beautiful family."

"Thank you."

"We never made stuff like this, my family and I. Well, we did, but... I was little, you know?" The admission surprised me. The words had slipped out like blood from a wound I didn't know I had. Looking at that Christmas card was like staring through a window into a life I'd never lived: one where families posed together because they actually wanted to be near each other, where holidays meant something more than an excuse to get drunk and avoid conversation. Thomas had built something *real* here, something that would outlast him.

All I'd built was a body count and a debt I couldn't pay.

***

Later, I sat alone on Thomas's sofa, watching the clock tick past 3 A.M. Thomas argued with his robed and distraught wife, Deborah, at the head of their staircase. I couldn't help but eavesdrop:

"It's just for the night," Thomas insisted.

"You don't even know the first thing about this guy!"

"Look, I just... I think he's into something..."

"So you bring him here. With your son sleeping upstairs."

"You didn't talk to him."

"I don't need to, Thomas. This is our home. There's certain luxuries that come with having one—like sleeping peacefully. There's *boundaries*."

"He's hurt. Badly. I'm taking him in at eight, and that's it. You won't even be awake."

"Did you not, for one second, actually question how he came to end up the way he is?"

"He's just a kid, Deb. A kid that looks like he's been through Hell. And he's safe here."

"Are we?"

The question hung in the air like smoke, poisoning the atmosphere of their perfect home. Deborah was right to be afraid: I was a walking *plague*. Even now, sitting in their living room trying to play the grateful victim, I was calculating exit strategies and wondering if I'd have to hurt them to get what I needed. *That's* what I'd become: someone who considered violence against good people as a viable option.

"I... *Yes*—"

"You want him down there? Then you can stay down there with him."

Deborah slammed the bedroom door. Thomas sighed and returned to the living room.

"Look, Mr. Berkshire, I can just go. I don't wanna cause any trouble." I started to rise, but my body protested with sharp pain.

"It's Thomas. And you'll stay. Pay my wife no mind. I'll bring you to my office in the morning and we'll have a better look."

I smiled gratefully. "Thanks. I really appreciate this."

Thomas nodded and walked to his bar. "Want a drink?"

"I'm fine."

"Doctor's orders." He poured two whiskies, neat, and handed me one. "Just a few sips."

He retrieved a cigarette case from a drawer, lighting one with a practiced motion. "What kind of doctor are you?" I asked. "You smoke and you won't take no for an answer."

"A doctor that knows what's good for the human condition, not just the vessel." Thomas took a long drag. "Seriously, drink up. Nascent alcoholism would be the least of your problems."

I smiled and sipped the whiskey, feeling it burn pleasantly down my throat. "A lot of things have become the least of my problems."

"You're probably wondering, so I'll just get this out of the way." Thomas set his drink down. "I found the blow. And the money. A good deal of it was actually floating in my swimming pool. Obviously, some of it's wet, but what I managed to find was mostly intact."

My stomach dropped. "When?"

"Right after I sat you down. You were out for a while."

"So..."

"Well, it's yours. Of course, I have nothing to do with it, nor do I *want* anything to do with it

"Where is it?"

Thomas pointed to a storage area beneath the staircase. I shot to my feet, ignoring the pain.

"But, if you'll humor an aging gent... let me tell you something first."

I stopped, our eyes meeting across the room.

Slowly, I sat back down.

"In life, a man is given a few real choices. Some less." Thomas leaned forward, his expression serious. "Now, I don't know what went wrong to lead *you* to *that*. In fact, I don't know the first thing about you, apart from what I recovered in that bag. But what I do know is, right now, you have a choice. You can spend the night. Get some sleep. And in the morning, we'll get some coffee in you, maybe some pancakes, and properly deal with things. Or, and I don't advise this, you can take that bag and leave. Go back to whatever it is you're running from."

"What if there isn't a choice?" I asked, the weight of Don's deadline pressing on me.

"There always is. You just don't see it. Or you refuse to."

"Look, I get that you're a do-gooder. Maybe you're one of those people that takes in strays. But you and I both know that the last thing you actually want to see when you wake up tomorrow is me, hanging around. This isn't your problem."

"That's where you're wrong. The second you rolled into my life it became my problem."

"That's not how people think—"

"People? Or just the people you find yourself hanging around?"

His words landed with unexpected resonance, hitting me like a freight train. I sat in silence, turning them over in my mind. Thomas was offering me something I'd forgotten existed: a choice that wasn't between two different kinds of destruction. For months, every decision had been about damage control: which lie to tell, which person to betray, which moral boundary to cross next.

But here was someone suggesting I could simply stop, could choose human connection over criminal enterprise, could wake up tomorrow without blood on my hands. It was a foreign concept, like being offered the chance to breathe underwater. Part of me wanted to believe it was possible. The rest of me knew that Don Silva was waiting at 8 A.M. with a bullet that didn't care about redemption arcs or second chances.

Thomas extinguished the cigarette and stood up. "For what it's worth, I really do hope to see you in the morning."

I watched him walk down the hallway. "I'll be in the guest bedroom. Bathroom's two doors down to your left if you'd like to wash up. I left a tracksuit on the kitchen table. It doesn't fit me anymore—in fact, it may never have—but you might have better luck."

I cleared my throat. "Hey, thanks. Again."

I meant it.

He smiled. "Good night, Marcus."

"Night," I replied softly.

***

Time had become my enemy, each tick of Thomas's antique clock a countdown to my execution.

Outside, Los Angeles slept fitfully: the city of dreams turning over in bed, muttering the names of people it had chewed up and spat out. I'd become one of those names, another cautionary tale about what happened when you confused ambition with wisdom. The irony wasn't lost on me: I'd come here to become somebody, and I had. Just not someone worth saving.

In the bathroom, I showered, letting hot water cascade over my battered body. Each new bruise and cut revealed itself under the harsh bathroom light: a map of bad decisions and worse consequences.

As I dried off, my phone vibrated on the counter. UNKNOWN CALLER. I answered.

"Marcus Graves..." Freddy's voice slithered through the speaker.

"Freddy."

"You're a hard man to pin down."

"Well, Freddy, you're just not my type."

"Funny. You know who I did find, though?"

My blood ran cold. "What?"

"My father had cancer, too. In hindsight, I probably should've just put him out of his misery. All that shit they pump into you, you're really better off dead."

"Where are you?"

"Hermosa. Little out of the way, but it is beautiful. So is that girl of yours. Well, *ex*-girl. I clocked her rebound a few minutes ago. Bit of a limp-dick but definitely an improvement. Actually, I can see her right now, smoking a cigarette on her parents' terrace. Alone. What kind of asshole makes a pretty girl smoke by herself?"

"If you touch her, I'll fucking kill you."

"You had your shot, bucko."

"Freddy, this is bigger than you and me. The cartel's gonna come for you. When you sold their product, you signed your own death warrant. I've made them millions and they're waiting to kill me as we speak, so don't think you have any sort of fucking leverage

"But I *do*, Marcus... I do. In fact, I'm looking at it right now." His smug satisfaction poured through the phone. I made a last-ditch attempt to genuinely, truly level with him:

"They'll kill everybody. You, the girls, your family."

"Fuck you! You know I might have brain damage, asshole? Huh? YOU KNOW HOW FUCKING HARD YOU HIT ME?!"

"Freddy—"

"*Don't*. Don't say another fucking word, you little mongrel. Flashing your puppy dog eyes around, trying to find a place to belong."

I took a deep breath, changing tactics.

"Freddy, you can have the money. I really don't care anymore. Where can I meet you?"

There was a pause.

Then, finally: "Did you talk to anybody about this?"

"No. Where can I meet you?"

"There's a pull-in south of the pier with a walkway to the beach."

"I know it."

"Thirty minutes."

I hung up, staring at my reflection in the mirror. The bruised, battered face looking back at me was a stranger's.

I put on the tracksuit Thomas had left for me and silently made my way to the front door. As I reached for the doorknob, a small voice stopped me.

"Are you really in trouble? I heard my dad saying that."

Norman sat at the foot of the stairs in SpongeBob pajamas, his eyes serious beyond his years.

"Yeah, I am," I said, low. "Trying to get out of it, though."

"Good luck."

We shared a look, something unspoken passing between us. In Norman's eyes, I saw the kind of trust I'd murdered in myself years ago: the belief that adults were fundamentally good, that the world made sense, that tomorrow would be better than today. He was looking at me like I was worth worrying about, like my survival mattered to the universe. It was the same way Stephanie used to look at me, back when I was still pretending to be human.

I wanted to tell him to stop, to save that faith for someone who deserved it. Instead, I just nodded and let him believe in a version of me that had died somewhere between the strip club and Trevor's house.

I slipped out into the night.

***

Ricky's truck sat a few houses down from Trevor's, untouched by the chaos. I found his keys and slid behind the wheel.

In the silence, tears came.

Then I was sobbing, violent and raw.

How many lives had I ruined? Cut short? And for what—to feel like a man? To serve some murdering conglomerate? Money?

It wasn't just tragic. It was unforgivable.

My friend would be alive right now if not for my chaos. Instead he was dead while I ran with blood money. Now Stephanie was in the crosshairs of two armed psychopaths with nothing left to lose.

I thought about the gun. Side of the head. Quick.

No.

Stephanie. My dad. Rocco. Even Greg. They didn't deserve what would happen next.

This was my mess.

Hell could wait.

I turned the key.
The engine caught.
This was it.

14

THE BALLAD OF MARCUS GRAVES

"It's been thirty-two minutes!" Freddy spat, mouth full of cotton. "Who the fuck does this kid think he is?"

"I don't like this, man. Shit's getting kinda spooky," Maurice observed from behind the wheel, apparently having already moved past the part of the evening where he'd chased a man through a cliffside home with a twelve-gauge.

"Oh. I'm sorry, Maurice. Maybe if you hadn't missed with a fucking buckshot at point-blank range, we wouldn't have to do *this*."

"It's not that much money, man. You're trippin'."

"I'm—*Get the fuck outta here*. Would you *look* at my face!" Freddy's bandaged face contorted with rage. "Anyway, the money's the least of my concerns. It's the principle. You know what that word means?"

Maurice glared at him.

"Look, he's showing up any moment now. You want to pop him or should I?" Freddy asked, fingering his gun.

Maurice ignored him, staring straight ahead, jaw set in a way that suggested Freddy had genuinely hurt his feelings with the "principle" comment.

"Hello? Anybody home?" Freddy waved a hand in front of his face. "Silent treatment, huh? *Fine*. I'll fucking do it, and happily at that. In fact, I can't wait."

Maurice shook his head.

Waves crashed. They sat in tense silence.

Finally, an engine sounded in the distance.

Maurice jumped.

Freddy perked. "You hear that?"

They were about to feel it.

I floored the accelerator, Ricky's modded-up truck barreling toward them like Christine off three Monsters and a shot of test.

The grille guard was about to prove its once ambiguous worth beautifully.

BOOM! Metal screamed against metal as I T-boned the Escalade from the driver's side at seventy MPH. The impact sent their vehicle tumbling down the beach embankment in an explosion of glass, rolling before coming to rest upside down on the sand.

I stepped out, leaving the engine running. The .45 felt light and charged in my hand as I slid down the embankment.

Freddy crawled out from under the wreckage, one leg dragging behind him. Maurice was nowhere to be seen.

"There's nothing out there for you," I shouted over the surf, watching Freddy crawl toward the tide.

He ignored me, desperate for the ocean like it might save him. I put my foot in his spine.

"It's over, Freddy."

I aimed the gun, but before I could decide whether to pull the trigger, Freddy flipped himself over.

His throat had been cut by glass in the crash. He clawed at me, grasping my legs as he gasped for air, blood pumping out with each heartbeat.

"Help me... Hel..." The words gurgled in his throat.

I stood there, watching as life drained from him. In just ten seconds, his eyes went from terror to ease to bliss to nothing. His hands fell away from my legs. The tide crept in, lapping at his head, already beginning to wash away the blood that pooled around him.

I tucked my gun away and walked back up the beach without looking back. Some deaths you cause, others you merely witness. I wasn't sure which category this fell into, though I had a feeling God hadn't made them mutually exclusive.

When I reached Stephanie's parents' house, it was nearly dawn. The sky was turning from black to indigo along the horizon, the first hints of sunrise scaring off the stars.

She opened the door slowly, her face a mask of concern and wariness. I stepped inside, my body aching with each movement.

"Marcus, what the fuck is going on?" Her voice was jagged, something sitting unevenly between furious and maternal and terrified.

"Is my dad okay?"

"He fell asleep hours ago."

"Are *you* okay?"

"I mean, I-I think, why wouldn't—*Jesus*, what happened to you? Let me take you to the hospital—"

"I'm about to tell you something. And you're not gonna understand but I just need you to trust me."

"What is it?"

"How much gas do you have in your car?"

"Half a tank. Why?"

"Grab a travel bag from upstairs. Take only what you need. And drive—drive as far away from here as possible."

Stephanie's eyes narrowed. "*Marcus.*"

"You need to leave. People are gonna be looking for me, which means they'll look for you, too."

"Why would they do that?"

"Because that's just what they do."

A loaded silence fell between us.

"If it's really come to this," she finally said, her voice careful, "then maybe you should just turn yourself in. They can't get to you if you're between a set of bars in a building full of cops."

"Not happening. And even if I did, you don't think they have people in there?"

Stephanie shook her head, sadness and disappointment etched on her face. "Marcus, you're the smartest person I've ever met. How is this a surprise to you? This was *always* gonna happen. And I tried. I tried so hard to pull you away, but you just..." She trailed off as tears broke, but she kept going. "You went deeper. You just kept going deeper and I—"

"Steph—"

"I STAYED." Her voice hit the walls, coming out of her like a rebar through concrete and rattling my chest. She hadn't even screamed like that the night she caught me with Roxy.

I looked at her. Held her eyes for a long second because I owed her that much. Then I said the only thing left to say—the truest thing, and perhaps the most pathetic.

"I was good at it." My voice broke on the admission.

Stephanie's tears stopped. Her face went flat, and her voice dropped to the register of a mother explaining why you can't keep the stray you dragged home.

"Marcus, you would've been good at *anything*."

"She's not going anywhere." Greg's voice came from the stairs. He stood there in boxer shorts and a t-shirt, arms crossed.

"And, just so you know, I called the cops. You got about five minutes."

Stephanie started to say something, but I cut her off.

"It's fine. Don't worry about it."

I opened the door and looked back at her one last time. "I'm sorry. For everything."

The door closed on whatever she might have said in response.

Back in the truck, I pulled away from the curb and floored it, leaving Hermosa Beach behind.

I had one more appointment to keep.

15

ANIMALS

Don Silva waited at the construction site overlooking the city, the morning light casting long shadows across the dirt lot.

His black Escalade gleamed, The Man in Black and two other enforcers flanking him like dark sentinels. The city spread out below us like a circuit board, all lights and connections and the promise of electric possibility. From up here, you couldn't see the human wreckage, couldn't smell the desperation or hear the sound of dreams being fed into industrial shredders. It looked beautiful, manageable, like something you could understand if you just had the right vantage point. But I'd learned that height was just another form of distance, another way to avoid seeing what you were really part of.

I killed the engine and took a deep breath, steadying myself. My backpack, containing what remained of the money and cocaine, felt ridiculously heavy as I approached them.

"I'd be lying if I said I wasn't a little impressed," Don remarked, his eyes coldly assessing my battered state.

"Brought the team, huh?" I nodded toward his men.

"Perhaps another time we can speak in private."

"There's not gonna be another time." I threw the bag at Don's feet with finality.

Don signaled to an enforcer to count it. "Why else would you come?"

"I settle my debts."

"Good boy," he smiled, patronizing.

"It's all there."

"We'll make sure of that. Once we do, I'd suppose that means we're back in business."

I looked at him incredulously. "It's all that simple to you?"

"Transactions are inherently simple."

"How about murder?"

"For better or worse, it's men like myself that keep this ugly little rock spinning."

"More like running in place."

Don's expression hardened slightly. "Your partner wasn't personal."

"He was my FRIEND!" The words tore from me, raw with emotion.

"He used you. You were nothing but a pawn to him. But I see you for who you are, Marcus. You're a warrior. Buddy was nothing but a cowardly peasant in shiny armor. A fool."

Part of me knew it was true. For years, I'd been operating on calculation and survival instinct, emotions blunted by necessity and cocaine. But standing there, confronted with Don's surgical dissection of my relationship with Buddy, I felt something crack open inside my chest: not just loss, but the terrible recognition that I'd loved someone incapable of loving me back. Buddy had been using me from day one, and I'd been so desperate to matter to someone that I'd mistaken exploitation for friendship.

"With me, you stand a chance to fulfill your potential," Don went on, his voice taking on an almost fatherly tone. "Now, where do we stand?"

"There is no *we*, Don. After this, my services will no longer be available to you, or anybody like you. Because I don't work for you. In fact, I never did."

"This is how you repay my mercy?"

"Fuck you, Don. You know, for a while, I took this pride in what I had become. I thought I was something. But you know what I realized? I was never anything but a selfish, arrogant thug, high on false glory. A little shit. I ruined lives in the name of your people's greed. And I'm done playing on your behalf. I don't want any more part of your destruction, your suffering. Because you're gonna die. Just like the rest before you. These people next to you? They're not your men. They're wild animals. And you know what wild animals do, Don? They go where the wind blows. And they eat whatever falls."

Don and I held each other's gaze for a long moment. Then I nodded, done with this chapter of my life, and turned back to the truck.

That's when I heard the gun cock behind me. I halted, but didn't turn around.

"Such wasted talent."

I looked back at him now, seeing the gun aimed at my chest.

"Did you really think you could just walk away?"

My shoulders dropped. "Honestly? No."

"You could've been a king."

"And you could've been aborted. You going to shoot me with that thing, Don, or can I go? I've got drinks with your mother later."

His grip tightened, finger closing on the trigger.

I closed my eyes at the last second.

The gunshot rang out.

I flinched, but felt no impact. Another shot, then a third. I opened my eyes and looked down at my unharmed body, confusion washing over me.

I turned to see The Man in Black standing over the bodies of the two enforcers, a silenced pistol hanging at his side. Don Silva, shot through the neck, crumpled to the ground, choking on his own blood.

The Man in Black turned his gun toward me. I stood frozen, our eyes locked. Then, unexpectedly, he flipped the gun around, offering me the handle.

I moved forward but shook my head, refusing the weapon. We both looked down at Don, who was frantically trying to stem the flow of blood from his neck wound. With his free hand, he groped for his fallen gun. I kicked it away and crouched beside him.

I wrapped my hands around his throat and squeezed. Don clawed at my wrists, but the blood loss had already stolen his strength. It took less time than I expected. His eyes went wide, then wider, then nowhere. His head sank to the ground and that was it.

The Man in Black retrieved the backpack from beside Don's body. He reached in and pulled out several stacks of bills, which he tossed to me.

"Go back East. Change your name. Then consider a long-term vacation. The Maldives, maybe. They don't extradite. It's quite pretty, too."

"Why did you save me?" I asked, bewildered by this unexpected turn.

"I didn't. As I told you, a man is only as good as his principles."

He zipped the backpack and walked to the Escalade.

"What if I wanted to die?" I called after him.

The Man in Black paused, a smile touching his lips. "Nobody wants to die."

He threw the bag into the passenger seat and drove away, leaving me alone with the dead.

I stood there for a while.

Then I picked up the money and walked back to the truck.

EPILOGUE

Union Station hummed with the energy of departures and arrivals, lives intersecting briefly before continuing on separate trajectories. I approached the ticket agent, sunglasses hiding my bruised face, a Dodgers cap pulled low over my eyes. The disguise was pathetic: a child's idea of going incognito, like sunglasses could hide what I'd become or a baseball cap could erase the dried blood on my neck.

"Philadelphia, please."

On the train, I watched Los Angeles recede, the city of broken dreams growing smaller through the window as we passed over the concrete-lined river and into the sprawling suburbs. A laugh escaped me, part relief, part disbelief that I had survived. The sound surprised me, hollow and brittle, like something broken trying to remember what wholeness felt like.

The city had changed me, consumed parts of me I would never get back. But as the landscape shifted from urban to rural, I felt a weight lift. There was still a chance for something else, something that didn't end in blood and regret. The optimism felt strange, like wearing clothes that belonged to someone else.

Marcus Graves, the pre-law student who'd arrived in Los Angeles with dreams and a work-study job, had believed in second chances. But that Marcus was as dead as Buddy, as dead as Trevor, as dead as everyone else I'd left in my wake. This was something different: not redemption, but the simple biological imperative to keep breathing, to see what came next.

Maybe that was enough.

Months later, I crafted a postcard. I addressed it to Stephanie's new place in Hollywood. I'd been keeping tabs, just to make sure she was safe. The same skills I'd used to destroy lives were now deployed to protect the one person who'd tried to save mine. Her guardian angel and her greatest threat simultaneously, watching from the shadows to ensure the monsters I'd attracted never found her.

It was the least I could do. And probably the most.

I didn't write anything on it. What was there to say?

Sorry for almost getting you murdered?

Thanks for taking my giant dog?

Some things are better left unspoken. The postcard was all I could offer, a sign that I was alive, that I had escaped, that I was trying to be better than the man she'd known.

I imagined her in her apartment in Los Angeles, sitting cross-legged on her bed in those sweats from H&M, staring at the postcard with that quizzical, severe look of hers. Then the jingle of a collar pulling her attention to the doorway, where Rocco stood, panting and awaiting permission to enter.

She would drop the card, her face lighting up. "Come here, sweet boy. Come here."

Rocco would bound onto the bed as only Rocco could, rolling over shamelessly for a belly rub, and as her fingers sank into his fur, a smile would spread across her face, completely untainted by the shadow of what might have been, what would never be, what *could* never be.

Some stories don't get happy endings. Sometimes you just get to walk away with your head and start over.

But in a city of angels and demons, dreams and nightmares, sin and salvation, and just about every goddamn thing in between, keeping my head didn't sound half bad. And if I'd learned anything from this bleached metropolis, a little rebrand might be just what I needed.

If only I'd ever made it to Philly.

ABOUT THE AUTHOR

J ACK CHASE is an American novelist, short story writer, essayist, and the founder of Abbycat Group & Publishing Brands. He is known for *Made in America: or The Tragedy of Billy Castle and Unexpected Absolution of Dean Willis* and *The Bastard of Taylor's End*. He has been regarded for his storytelling range, morally complex characters, and prolific output, releasing twelve books in his first year of publishing.